TIME TO PREY

BOOKS BY RAEGAN TELLER

Murder in Madden

The Last Sale

Secrets Never Told

The Fifth Stone

Time to Prey

TIME TO PREY

Raegan Teller

Raegan Teller (signature)

Pondhawk Press LLC
Columbia, South Carolina

Pondhawk Press LLC
PO Box 290033
Columbia, SC 29229
www.PondhawkPress.com

Publisher's Note: This is a work of fiction. Names, characters, places, and incidents are a product of the author's imagination. Locales and public names are sometimes used for atmospheric purposes. Any resemblance to actual people, living or dead, or to businesses, companies, events, institutions, or locales is completely coincidental.

ISBN 978-0-9979205-8-1

"Truth is like the sun.
You can shut it out for a time,
but it ain't goin' away."

– Elvis Presley

CHAPTER 1

Today began like a normal day for Enid Blackwell, managing editor for the *Tri-County Gazette,* in Madden, South Carolina. She approved the last article for this week's edition written by a young woman fresh out of school with a new journalism degree. From what Enid could tell, the reporter, Mia Olson, had potential, so she likely wouldn't hang around long. The good ones stayed long enough to be mentored by Jack Johnson, the owner of the weekly paper and then, usually with Jack's help, they found a better-paying job at a daily rag. She couldn't blame them. The newspaper industry was gasping its last breath, and reporters had to find a good spot while there were some left.

The majority of fresh journalism graduates never actually work at a print newspaper. Instead, they go into corporate communications positions and other roles. It was too early to determine how long Mia would last. In the meantime, she was writing some good pieces, which made Enid's job easier.

A knock on her office door interrupted her thoughts. "Hey, Jack, come on in."

"Just thought I'd check on my favorite editor. Need any help finishing this week's edition?"

Enid smiled, because this was a daily ritual with Jack since she filled the editing position while he took chemo treatment. "You always seem disappointed when I tell you the paper is ready to go."

Jack smiled. "Yeah, I guess I am a bit. You know, I'm feeling a little useless these days."

Enid pointed toward the chair in front of her desk. "Do you have a minute to talk?"

"Sure," he said as he took a seat. "What's on your mind?"

Enid straightened the stack of papers on her desk to buy a few seconds of time. "Mia has the potential to be a good reporter. At least I think so. But you might want to spend some time with her."

"I'm happy to, but I'm not sure I can help her any more than you can."

"But you have experience with the *Chicago Tribune* and more experience than I had with the Associated Press. She has ambitions you can address better than I."

Jack slapped his palms on his thighs. "Sure. Happy to." He paused. "But that's not what this is about, is it?"

Enid laughed. "That's the wonderful thing about close friends, but it's also a bit invasive." She straightened the stack of papers again. "I'm so happy you're cancer free now. When you got the diagnosis more than a year ago, I was so worried."

"Were you worried about me or about stepping into the editor role?"

"Both, to be honest."

"This isn't what you want to do with your life. Is that it?"

"I won't leave you hanging. If you're not ready to become managing editor again, I'll keep it for a little while longer."

Jack leaned forward. "Dear Enid, you are more wonderful than I can tell you. And I know you have only tolerated this job for my sake." He sat back in his chair. "And to be honest, I'm getting a little bored with just hanging around getting in your way."

"Whew. Then you're ready to be editor again?"

Jack stood and slapped his hands on the desk. "Yes! You are respectfully fired as managing editor. But I'm offering you your old job as senior reporter. Do you accept?"

Enid tapped her pen on the desk. "Maybe."

Jack's smile disappeared. "Come on, we're a team. You wouldn't leave the paper." He paused, "Would you?"

Enid smiled. "Not yet, at least." But I had you going for a minute, didn't I?"

Jack cocked his head and smiled. "Yes, you scared me to death." He stood to leave as Ginger, the office manager, burst into Enid's office.

"There's a girl missing," she said, waving her hands in the air.

"Missing?" Enid asked. "Who? Where?"

"It's that girl who won the scholarship to Duke."

Enid pointed to her computer screen. "I was just looking at the article Mia did on her last week. Her name is Winifred Alexia Tucker."

"Well, that's a mouthful," Ginger said. "Sounds like old money too."

Enid nodded. "According to Mia's article, Winifred comes from a prominent Bowman County family. Her mother's family made their fortunes in cotton and then tobacco. Now they're into soybeans and floriculture." She turned to Ginger. "Do you know anything else about her disappearance?"

Ginger shook her head. "Nada."

"I'll contact Mia and let her know," Enid said to Jack.

"Good. I'll see what I can find out from my sources."

After Jack and Ginger left Enid's office, she called Mia. No answer, so she left a message. "Call me when you get this. Your scholarship girl is missing."

A moment later, Enid's personal cell phone rang. She didn't recognize the caller.

A voice that sounded electronically altered responded: "Enid, I've been wanting to meet you. I admire your work, and I want to help advance your career."

"Who is this?"

The laugh sounded disembodied: "Your biggest fan. I hope you like the gift I've given you."

Enid wondered briefly if her ex-husband Cade was playing a joke on her. Yet, there was something in the caller's tone that was menacing. For all his faults, Cade would never intentionally try to scare her. Besides, he was still in London on assignment with the Associated Press, and based on their last conversation, he didn't have time to play games with her.

"I'm not in the mood for prank calls. Don't call here again." How did he get her private number?

The office phone rang, and she recognized Mia's cell number. "Thanks for calling me back."

"I just got the news about Winifred's disappearance. I'm going to see the parents now. Maybe they'll give me some information."

"Alright. Let me know if you find out anything new. We've got two days until the paper goes out, so if you can get me an update by tomorrow evening, I'll include it." Enid paused. "Oh, and just so you'll know, Jack is taking back his editor's job, but I'll fill him in."

"What are you going to do now?"

"I'll go back to being senior reporter."

"Oh." Mia's voice was low and soft. "I'm sure that will be easier for you, but I enjoyed working with you."

"Thanks. And don't worry, I just told Jack you have a lot of potential. He's a great mentor with a lot of experience and contacts. He can help you far more than I can." Enid didn't wait for Mia to respond. "Just keep me posted on the Tucker girl."

After the call, Enid's mind drifted back to the strange call she had gotten. What kind of gift was the caller referring to? Maybe it was a female. Hard to tell with the altered voice. Enid had that feeling again, the one Jack called her reporter's instinct. That sensation that began in the pit of her stomach wasn't infallible, but more often than not, it preceded something that wasn't good.

CHAPTER 2

Mia called Winifred's mother several times but got no answer, so she decided to drive to their house. When she arrived, two sheriff's deputies' cars were in the driveway. So far, no sign of a newspaper reporter from the *State* or any other paper. Maybe she could get a slight jump on them. Working for a weekly paper had its benefits, but it also meant smaller, less newsworthy stories, mostly of local interest. She grew up in Boston but always wanted to live in a small town. While she would likely move on to bigger things later, she wanted to do her best and to be remembered for her hard work and excellent writing while working for the *Tri-County Gazette*.

When Mia walked up to the wraparound porch encircling the huge white house, a deputy stopped her. "Ma'am, you can't go in there."

"But I know the family."

"Are you immediate family?" he asked.

"No, but . . ."

"Let her through please," a woman's voice called out. Mrs. Tucker was holding the screen door open. "She's okay."

The deputy threw his hands up and backed out of Mia's path.

Mia followed Mrs. Tucker into the house. "I'm sorry to barge in on you, but I heard the news and was just devastated. Is there anything I can do to help?"

Mrs. Tucker sat in a large, overstuffed chair and motioned for Mia to sit on the sofa. "You obviously can't report on any of this. Do I have your word?" Her large blue eyes were glistening with tears.

"I'm not here as a reporter," Mia said, which wasn't exactly true but partially so. "I really like Winnie."

A slight smile. "Winnie likes you too. As an only child, Winnie always wanted a big sister. That's how she feels about you." Another hint of a smile. "In fact, after you talked with her, she declared she wanted to be a reporter."

Mia's disappointment with not being able to do a story about Winifred's disappearance was replaced with pride. *People first, story later,* Jack told her when he hired her. However, he also admitted his advice wouldn't help her much once she left for a bigger paper. "Do you mind telling me what happened? Off the record, of course."

Mrs. Tucker gripped the handkerchief in her hands so tightly her knuckles were white. She appeared to be gathering her thoughts. "Winnie is everything to us." She stopped to clear her throat. "She could have easily become a spoiled child, but she is just the opposite. As you learned from her interview, she does volunteer work and always puts others first." She looked directly at Mia. "But you know all that. My husband worked all the time. I'm sure that's what killed him." She glanced around the room. "I need to sell this place, but Winnie loves it so. We have a couple horses here, although Winnie is the only one who rides. Anyway, I've just never been attracted to horses the way Winnie is. We have a young man that helps us manage the stable. Winnie said she was going to walk to the barn to ride Hero, that's her favorite, a Morgan gelding, if you're into breeds and such."

After a period of silence during which Mrs. Tucker appeared to be lost in thought, Mia spoke. "I love horses, but I don't know much about them. What happened after she fed Hero?"

Mrs. Tucker looked up at Mia. "I'm sorry. This is all just too much for me." She paused. "Winnie never came back from the barn."

"You said you have a person who helps out. Did he see anything?"

"Chad is his name. He said he saw Winnie leave the barn to walk back here."

"Is the barn right out back?" Mia was hoping she could go check it out.

"No, my late husband insisted that we not have the barn too close to the house. You know, in case of smells and such. It's a little way down that dirt road near the house. Chad lives in a room behind the barn."

"Does Winnie usually walk to the barn?"

"Oh, yes. She's quite a walker. Loves to amble through the woods. She especially likes walking the path to the river."

"Was it dark when she left?"

"It was dusk. It gets dark earlier now, you know." Mrs. Tucker gazed out the window as though she expected Winnie to come walking up to the house any moment.

"I know the sheriff's office is doing everything they can, but would you mind if I talked with Chad?"

Mrs. Tucker looked puzzled. "Well, I suppose it's alright. But please don't write about any of this. I don't want to put Winnie in danger."

"I promise I won't write a thing without your permission. But when she's found safe, I'd like to do a follow-up article, if you don't mind."

Mrs. Tucker nodded.

"I'll just walk down to the barn now." Mia stood to leave. "Please let me know if I can do anything to help."

"You're welcome to drive if you'd prefer. It's a dirt road but wide enough for a car."

Mia glanced at her two-inch heels. "That's probably a good idea. Please let me know if, I mean when, Winnie shows up. I'm sure she'll be fine."

• • •

The dirt road to the barn was full of potholes. Mia drove slowly, dodging them, until she reached a large wooden barn. It was a big structure and well-maintained, just like the house and the rest of the property. Clearly, the Tuckers had money.

Mia parked her car beside the barn. As she was walking toward the back room where Mrs. Tucker said Chad stayed, Mia heard a voice.

"Can I help you?" A young man, looking to be about late twenties came out of the barn and approached her.

"I'm Mia, a friend of Mrs. Tucker. I also work for the *Tri-County Gazette*, but I'm not here as a reporter, just a friend. Are you Chad?"

"A reporter? Maybe I better not talk to you."

"You're welcome to call Mrs. Tucker and confirm it with her. I just left the house."

Chad turned and walked a few feet away, as he pulled his cell phone from his back pocket. After a brief conversation, he walked back to Mia. "She says you're okay."

"Look, I know you've probably told your story a dozen times now, but can you tell me what happened? I'd like to help the family any way I can."

Chad shrugged. "Nothing I can tell you or any of those sheriff's deputies. I didn't know Winnie was missing until Mrs. Tucker called me. After Winnie left, I was in the back room and I had my headphones on listening to music."

Mia turned around to look at the dirt road she had just driven on. Because of the bend in the road, the house was not visible from here, only woods. "If it was nearly dark, that's a bit dangerous for a young lady to be out here walking alone."

Chad's forehead creased. "Why? This is all their property, and nothing has ever happened here."

Oh, the naivety of youth. "Did she have a boyfriend that you knew of?"

Chad's stance stiffened slightly. "I wouldn't know anything about her personal life. I just take care of the horses, get paid a little, and get free rent." He raised his palms. "Anything else is way above my pay grade."

Mia smiled. Chad was articulate and handsome. Why was he working at such a menial job?

"Is there anything else?" he asked. "I need to get back to work."

She gave him a business card. "If you think of anything else, maybe something you'd rather not tell the deputies, you can trust me. My cell number is on the card."

Chad nodded without comment and put the card in his pocket as he walked back into the barn.

CHAPTER 3

The *Tri-County Gazette* covered Bowman County and two surrounding counties. The paper's office was in Madden, a small but growing town about thirty minutes from Columbia, the capital city. A large distribution center was responsible for Madden's recent growth. Depending on who you asked and on what day, the town folks either welcomed the newcomers and the money they brought to the town or despised them.

When Enid got to the newspaper office in downtown Madden, Jack's pickup was already in the parking lot beside the old brick building. Enid knew he was excited about being editor again, and she was more than happy to give up the role. She was a reporter, not an administrator, although with years of corporate banking experience, she was more than qualified to manage both people and operations. But for now, she was content being a small-town reporter. Maybe later, she would consider moving on. But Jack had become her family, as she had only a few distant cousins remaining on the family tree.

She walked into the biggest office in the building, Jack's office. Since she never moved into it when she assumed the editor role, Jack's return was nearly seamless. "Good morning."

"Hey, you. Didn't hear you come in." They chatted a few minutes, then Jack asked, "Did you get an update from Mia?

I need something by end of day."

"No, I haven't. I assumed she would report to you since I told her you were managing editor again."

"You're right. I'll follow up with her." He smiled. "I guess you need a few stories to write."

A tingle of anticipation enveloped Enid. "To be honest, I couldn't wait to get out of the editor role. You're welcome to it."

"I know you'd like to handle the Winifred Tucker story, but I can't pull it from Mia midstream. I hope you understand."

"I wouldn't want you to. That wouldn't be fair."

"But I will suggest that she consult with you. I doubt Mia ever covered this sort of thing. The *State* and other dailies will be all over it today." He handed Enid some papers from his desk. "Here are a few other things we need to cover. Let me know if you want to talk about any of them. Mostly local stuff, you know, rising property taxes, three-car traffic jams in Madden." He laughed. "They should try living in Chicago. Oh, and don't try to get anything to me today. Thanks to your excellent editing, we've got plenty for this edition. I'm holding the space for the Tucker girl's story when I get Mia's update."

Enid went to her office and began making calls and doing some research for the articles Jack requested.

Later that day, Enid's personal cell phone rang as she sat at her desk. The number was tagged as an unknown caller. "Hello."

The now familiar mechanical voice responded: "I'm going to make you even more famous. Your career stock will rise, and you'll get offers you never dreamed of."

"Is this some kind of sick joke? Who are you, and how

did you get my phone number?" Without waiting for a reply, she ended the call just as Jack walked into her office.

"Everything okay?" he asked.

"Just another prank call. Did you reach Mia?"

"No. I've left several messages. That's not like her to ignore them."

An incoming text diverted her attention as she glanced at the phone. "It's from Mia." She tapped on the message to read it.

"Well?" Jack asked.

"This is strange. She says, 'Go ahead and write the story about Winifred Tucker's disappearance. You're the senior reporter.'"

Jack took the phone from Enid and read the message himself. "Since when does she get to make assignments. Text her back and tell her to call me. Now."

"It's also strange that she refers to her as Winifred Tucker. Mia has always called her Winnie in our conversations."

Jack threw up his hands. As he left Enid's office, he called over his shoulder. "Why did I come back?"

Enid replied to the text as Jack requested. But something just didn't feel right, especially after Mia failed to respond after nearly ten minutes. Enid picked up her leather tote and walked the few feet down the hallway to Jack's office. "I'm going to see Mia. I'll let you know what I find out."

"Thanks. And tell her I'm not happy."

Enid smiled. "Oh, I will."

CHAPTER 4

Enid had never been to Mia's residence but knew about the garage apartment she rented from Mrs. Putnam. The Putnams lived in a big house just inside the Madden city limits, so Enid decided to walk. It was a beautiful late November day.

When Enid arrived at the Putnam house, she saw the garage apartment at the rear. A Buick SUV was parked in the driveway, but there was no sign of Mia's aging Toyota Corolla hatchback. As Enid walked to the garage apartment, a woman, whom Enid assumed was Mrs. Putnam, walked from the backyard to greet her, a gardening hoe in hand.

"Hello, can I help you?"

"I work with Mia. We haven't heard from her today, so I came to make sure she's okay."

Mrs. Putnam leaned the hoe against the back of the house. "I've been concerned about her too. She usually lets me know when she's not going to be here." She smiled. "I worry about her, you know, being a young lady away from home. Mr. Putnam and I have tried to watch out for her."

"That's very kind of you. I know she appreciates it." Enid studied the garage apartment for any signs of life, but the shades were down. "When did you last see her?"

"She works from home a lot, but you probably know that. She's in and out during the day, doesn't go out much at night. I guess Madden night life isn't very exciting for a young person here away from her family and friends."

"Do you mind if I knock on her door?"

"I don't want to intrude on her, but I think that's a good idea." Mrs. Putnam followed Enid up the steep stairs leading to the apartment.

After knocking three times, Enid asked, "She might be inside sick or hurt. Do you mind checking?"

Mrs. Putnam's face reflected her disapproval. "I'm not sure about that. You see, we always assure our renters absolute privacy."

"I totally understand, but if I can't locate her, I'll have to report her missing, so the Madden police will be back here to check inside. Just so you'll know."

Mrs. Putnam looked distressed. "Well, I suppose I could check, but you'll have to stay out here."

Enid nodded and waited until Mrs. Putnam went into her house and then returned with the key to the apartment.

When Mrs. Putnam went inside, she closed the door behind her. A few minutes later, she came out. Enid was waiting on the small landing at the top of the stairs, barely big enough to hold two adults. "She wasn't there. It's a small place, but I checked the closet and bathroom. Everything was neat and in place. That's one thing I really like about Mia. She's so respectful of our property."

Enid reached into her tote and handed Mrs. Putnam a business card. "Thanks for checking. Please let me know if she returns or you hear from her."

• • •

Enid returned to the newspaper office and told Jack about her visit to the Putnam house. "I just came back to get my car. I'm going to visit the Tuckers myself. Maybe she texted me from there. I know she had developed a bond with Winnie, so she might be visiting with Mrs. Tucker."

Jack stood. "Come on. I'll go with you. I need to get out of here. Getting back into the day-to-day grind wasn't as easy as I thought."

"You'd better tell Ginger where we are. You know she'll be upset if we both disappear."

Jack smiled. "You're right about that. I'll meet you in the parking lot."

CHAPTER 5

While Enid drove to the Tucker house, Jack leaned his head back on the headrest. "Are you feeling okay?" Enid asked.

Jack answered without opening his eyes or moving his head. "Yeah, just a bit tired. Like I said, getting back into the saddle is more of a challenge than I thought it would be."

"Do you regret coming back?"

Jack sat up straight. "Oh, goodness no. I don't mean to sound like I'm complaining. It's just that . . ." He leaned his head back again. "You know, just an adjustment."

The navigation system instructed Enid to turn left off the secondary highway down a two-lane paved road lined with trees. "I've never been here. Have you?"

"Once, a while back. The house is somewhat isolated. The Tuckers bought a lot of land when it was cheap. I thought sure when Mr. Tucker died they would sell all or at least some of it, but Mrs. Tucker held on to all that acreage. She's got several people working for her who run the farm. I can't imagine what the upkeep and operational costs must be."

"Or the property taxes. All this is prime land for development now."

"Don't say that. I know it's true, but I'm not ready for our little piece of paradise to become housing developments."

They drove in silence until a dirt driveway leading to a

large house appeared on the left. "According to my GPS, this is it."

Jack raised his head and looked out the window. "Yep, that's it." He sat up and pulled down the visor mirror to brush his hair back. "I need a haircut."

Enid laughed. "Oh, I don't know. I kinda like that Brad Pitt look on you." She parked beside a Bowman County car. Before Jack and Enid could get to the front door, a deputy opened it and came out onto the porch. "Can I help you?" he asked.

Enid showed him her press pass. "Our reporter from the *Tri County Gazette* came here to talk to Mrs. Tucker and we're trying to find her."

"A lady reporter was here earlier, but she left hours ago."

"Deputy Graves," Jack said, looking at the name badge on his shirt pocket, "I knew your dad, Gerald. He was a fine man." He paused. "So you saw Mia leave here?"

The deputy softened his stance a bit. "Thank you for saying that about Dad." The deputy cleared his throat. "I saw her drive down to the barn, and I assumed she left after that."

"So there's another way that she could have taken from the barn?" Enid asked.

"I assume so. I never saw her come back this way."

Jack rubbed the back of his neck. "Well, here's the thing, you see. We've been trying to reach her, and that's why we drove over here, thinking maybe she was with Mrs. Tucker. Mia interviewed Mrs. Tucker and Winnie for an article on Winnie's scholarship. That was before Miss Tucker disappeared, of course."

Deputy Graves leaned in toward Jack and spoke in a low voice, as if someone might overhear them. "I heard Mrs.

Tucker got a message from her daughter. You know, after she went missing." He held up his hand. "You can't report any of this. I'm just telling you 'cause you knew Dad. Could be just a prank call though."

"We won't," Jack said. "Thanks for your help." He nodded toward the car, signaling to Enid they should leave.

"Thanks for your help, deputy," Enid said.

Jack and Enid walked back to the car in silence and neither of them spoke for nearly half a mile. "What's going on?" she asked.

"I have no idea." Jack pulled his cell phone from his pocket. "I'm going to try Mia again." He tapped on her number in his contacts list and put the call on speaker. It rang several times before her voicemail announced she was unavailable. "Mia, this is Jack. I'm here with Enid. We just left the Tucker house. Call me right away. We're concerned about you."

"I've got this sinking feeling that something is not right."

Jack nodded as he stared down the road. "Me too."

CHAPTER 6

Sitting at her desk at the newspaper office the next day, Enid stared at her computer screen, unable to concentrate. *Mia, where are you?* Enid jumped when Ginger tapped on her office door. "Sorry, I was lost in thought. Do you need something?"

Ginger sat in the chair across from Enid's desk. "This package came for you."

Enid looked at it. "There's no postage. How did it get here?" "Enid Blackwell" was written across the envelope with a black marker.

"It was leaning against the door when I opened the office this morning." Ginger handed the large brown padded envelope to Enid."

"Thanks. Have you heard from Mia?"

Ginger shook her head. "I'm worried. Jack says none of her articles have been turned in, which isn't like her at all."

"I know." Enid set the envelope aside to open later. "Have you checked the hospitals? Or with the sheriff's office?"

"Checked both. Nothing. Do you think we should file a missing person's report?"

"Get me her parents' number from her employee file, and I'll give them a call—unless Jack's already done it."

Ginger pulled a slip of paper from one of the many pockets of her cargo pants. "Here. He wants you to call and see what you can find out."

"Sure, no problem."

After Ginger left, Enid called the number. It was a little early to call her parents in Boston, but Enid didn't want to wait.

The phone rang only once before a man answered. "Hello."

"I'm Enid Blackwell, from the *Tri-County Gazette.*"

"Do you have news about Mia? I'm her father."

"Well, actually, no, I was calling to see if you had heard from her. I got the impression she stays in close contact with you."

Mia's father sobbed quietly. "I'm sorry, it's just that, yes, she checks in with us every day. You see, her mother isn't well at all. I had just looked up the phone number for the paper and was getting ready to call your office."

"I'm sorry to hear about your wife's health." Enid paused. "We need to report Mia's disappearance, if that's what it is, to the Bowman County sheriff's office. Just in case. Although I'm sure she's alright."

"Thank you for saying that, Ms. Blackwell, but I know something is wrong. You see, we got a package in the mail from South Carolina. It was addressed to us. I opened it, and it was the earrings we gave Mia for her graduation from college."

"I remember telling Mia how lovely they are. Expensive too, so why would she, or someone else, mail them to you?" Enid remembered the envelope that Ginger handed her. "Wait. Hold just a minute." She took a photo of the envelope. Opening it carefully, she reached inside and pulled out a small bundle wrapped in white tissue paper that had red hearts on it. She took another photo and used the tip of her pen to push the paper back. Inside was a pair of ladies' pink underwear. Someone had drawn a big heart on them with what looked like the same kind of black marker used to write Enid's name on the envelope.

"Are you there?" Enid heard Mia's father ask, as she picked up the phone.

Should she tell him and worry him even more? Maybe it was a sick joke someone was playing. But she had no right to withhold the information. "I got a package this morning. It was apparently hand-delivered and addressed to me personally. After you told me about your package, I remembered it and just opened it."

"Does it have anything to do with Mia?"

"I don't know. It's a woman's personal item of clothing."

"What do you mean?"

"It's a pair of panties, but I'm sure you wouldn't be able to identify it."

"But I know the label she wears. Her mother has me order items for her periodically. You see, on Mia's salary, no offense to the paper, she can't afford many of the things she was accustomed to here with us."

"No offense taken. Jack, her editor, and I both realize Mia's talent and that she'll be leaving us soon for a bigger paper."

"She wanted to work for Jack. She researched small papers and read all about him and his experience. She considered it an internship with him as her mentor. Mia said he would be back soon, which is why she took that job. Although, she told us several times how much she learned working for you. But back to the point. As far as I know, she wears only Tommy John underwear. She raves about the fit to her mother when they talk."

Enid had never known her own father and was surprised Mia's father had knowledge of his daughter's clothing labels. Enid looked at the panties from the envelope and her heart sank. "We need to notify the police."

CHAPTER 7

Before ending the call with Mia's father, Enid promised to stay in touch. She convinced him to stay with his bedridden wife rather than come to South Carolina and that if anything changed, they would be notified immediately.

She ran down the hall to Jack's office, where he was on the phone. "I need to talk to you now."

Looking puzzled, Jack apologized to the person on the other end. "I'm sorry, but there's something I have to handle right away. Call you back later." Jack hung up and looked at Enid. "What's wrong? Have you found Mia?"

She filled him in on her conversation with Mia's father and showed him the panties.

"What kind of sicko would do something like that? Maybe an ex-boyfriend? And why did he send them to you?"

"I don't know, but let's call Pete now. He'll know what to do."

Pete Barnes was the police chief of Madden, South Carolina. He was young and had held the job only a few years but was well respected in the community. Pete agreed to come over right away when he got Jack's call.

Since the police station was only a few doors down from the newspaper office, Pete was in Jack's office within a few minutes.

"Thanks for coming so quickly," Jack said.

"What's going on? It's not like you to panic."

"We have a missing reporter, Mia Olson."

"How do you know she's missing? Have you talked to anyone else, her friends or family?" Pete asked.

Jack nodded to Enid, signaling her to talk first.

"Since I seem to be involved, I'll tell you what I know," Enid said. "Mia did an article on a young woman, Winifred Tucker, who received a scholarship to Duke. As you know, the Tuckers are a prominent family here in Madden."

Pete nodded. "Go on."

"After Mia's story ran, we heard about Winnie's disappearance, so I left a message for Mia. We know she talked with Mrs. Tucker. Then I got a text from Mia, at least it was from her number, telling me to take the lead on the story."

"But you haven't talked with her?" Pete asked.

"No, we've been trying to find Mia, but she just vanished." Enid paused. "And then I got this." She handed the large brown envelope to Pete. "I'm afraid I've already contaminated it with my prints."

"No problem. We can print and eliminate you," Pete said. He pulled latex gloves from his pocket. "But I don't want to add mine. Anyone else handle it?"

"Ginger."

"We'll eliminate her too," Pete said. He carefully opened the tissue paper. "What the . . .?"

Jack spoke up. "And to further complicate the matter, Enid talked to Mia's father in Boston. They got a package with Mia's earrings in it."

"I'll need Mia's full name, her parents' contact information, and anything you have that might help us. I'll talk to the Bowman County sheriff, but I'm sure we'll involve SLED in this. The county is short a few people right now."

Enid remembered when Pete was a new police chief and

had no clue about calling in the South Carolina Law Enforcement Division, the state police who often got involved in complex cases.

"Also, give me her mobile number and local address," Pete said.

"I went to her apartment, and the landlady checked inside for me. I'll give you her information also."

"Any idea why the package was sent to you?" Pete asked.

Enid and Jack looked at each other and both shook their heads.

"I'll need to get a statement from you," Pete said to Enid. "Anything else either of you can think of that I need to know?"

Both Enid and Jack shook their heads. "Oh, wait," Enid said. "There was this strange phone call I got right before Mia went missing. It sounded like one of those electronically altered voices."

"You didn't tell me about that," Jack said. "What did the person say?"

"At the time, I assumed it was a prank call. The caller said he, or perhaps she, admired my work and wanted to help advance my career." Enid's hand flew to her mouth. "Do you think the caller is the same person who took Mia?"

"Did he call your cell phone or the office number?" Pete asked.

Enid's chest tightened. "My private cell number."

"Okay, let's get that statement from you right away," Pete said. "Follow me to the police station."

CHAPTER 8

No reporter wants to become the news. Enid was thinking about the implications of her situation when her cell phone rang. It was an international number she recognized. "Hello, Cade."

A familiar male voice responded, "Did I wake you?"

"No, it's a little after 8:00 am here. I'm at the office."

"Right, I forgot you're the workaholic." Cade Blackwell, Enid's ex-husband, worked for the Associated Press and was assigned to London for more than a year investigating irregularities related to the United Kingdom's exit from the European Union. BrexitGate, he called it. When the assignment ended, he requested to stay.

"How are you?" she asked. When Cade first left, they talked or texted a good bit. But as time passed, their contacts dwindled to a few texts now and then.

"Yeah, everything is great. In fact, that's why I'm calling."

"I assume you're still in London."

Cade's laughter crossed the ocean. "Yes, and I'm getting married."

Ever since their divorce a few years earlier, Enid prepared herself for this call. It wasn't that she wanted to get back together with Cade, but she had to admit she wasn't ready to let go completely. Their divorce was amicable and they vowed to remain friends, but Enid knew they would continue to drift apart, especially if he remarried.

"Enid, are you there?"

"Uh, yes, sorry. Of course, I'm happy for you. Very happy."

"Her name is Claire, and she owns a boutique in London. I know you'll just love her as much as I do."

"I'm sure I will. Well then, congratulations. When is the wedding?"

"More than likely it will be next year. I'm about to break a big story, and I can't stop to plan a wedding."

"So you'll stay in London after you're married?"

"Probably, since she has a business here. Wait, hold a minute."

Enid could hear bits of a muffled conversation, as if he had his hand over the phone.

"Hey, I'm back. Sorry, but I've got to run. We'll talk again later. 'Bye." And then he was gone.

Enid sat at her desk, staring at her cell phone. She wasn't overly surprised, and she wasn't sad. So what was she feeling? Before she could contemplate the answer, Ginger came into her office.

"Got a minute?"

"Sure." Enid put her cell phone down and focused on Ginger, who looked anxious.

"I just got a call for you. I think it was a man, but it was hard to tell. He said he wanted to leave you a message."

Enid was suddenly having trouble breathing. "What was it?"

"I repeated it, you know, just to make sure I had it right."

"Just tell me."

"He said to tell you Winnie and Mia are inseparable now, thanks to you."

Enid stiffened. "What does that mean?"

Ginger shrugged. "Beats me. Anyway, I've got the number he called from, and I'm trying to find out who it is. I'll let you know what I find out." As she walked out of Enid's office, she called out over her shoulder. "Weird, just weird."

CHAPTER 9

An hour later, Ginger returned to Enid's office. "Hey, sorry to bother you again, but I've got a call for you. You want to take it?"

"Who is it?" Enid asked.

"A reporter from the *State* newspaper."

"What did he want?"

In typical Ginger fashion, she put her hand on her left hip and cocked her body to one side. "Now if I knew that, I would have told you right off. He said he just needed for you to call him pronto." She handed Enid a bright pink message note.

"Okay. Thanks."

After Ginger left, Enid stared at the message, as if doing so would bring clarity to a day that was already unsettling. She returned the call on the office phone and punched in the number from the note when the if-you-know-your-party's-extension recording finished.

"Hey, Ty here."

"This is Enid Blackwell, I understand—"

Before she could finish, Ty said, "Hey, yeah, thanks for calling me back." He sounded young and eager, the way she remembered Cade when they were both stringers for the AP in their early years of marriage. "I'd like to set up a time to interview you. Now would be good for me, that is if you're free."

"Whoa, slow down a minute. What's this about? Why do you want to interview me?"

"Sorry, I guess I didn't explain myself very well. I'm working on Winifred Tucker's disappearance and the possible disappearance of one of your reporters. My source said Mia . . . What's her last name? Oh, here it is. Mia Olson works for you at the *Tri-County Gazette*. Is that right?"

Enid took a deep breath to steady her nerves. "First of all, Ty, we don't know that Mia is officially missing. And second, she was only temporarily working for me. Jack Johnson is the managing editor and Mia's boss."

"Whatever. I'd still like to talk to you."

"I'm sorry but I'm just not the person you need. You can contact Jack and see if he'll talk with you."

"But . . ." Ty paused briefly. "My source also said you had been contacted by a person of interest."

Ty was as irritating as he was determined and obviously had sources with inside information. "I see. Well, I get crank calls fairly often, and that's all I think that was. Your source is making something out of nothing. Now, if you don't mind, I need to get back to work."

"Wait, I know you are upset, but don't you want me to report it correctly?"

Enid laughed. "Professor Pearson."

"Excuse me?"

"That was one of the tactics he taught in journalism school to get people to talk. Now, I've really got to go."

After she ended the call, she walked a short distance down the hallway to Jack's office. He rarely shut his door, but it was closed now. Enid walked to Ginger's desk at the front of the office. "Do you know if Jack's in his office or if he has visitors?"

Ginger leaned forward and spoke in a soft, conspiratorial tone. "He's meeting with a guy he knew at the *Chicago Tribune*."

"So he's talking with an old friend. Why are you whispering?"

"I think there's more to it than that. Jack asked me to pull some financial reports—" She stopped as Jack and the man walked out toward Ginger's desk. The man put out his hand and shook Jack's vigorously. "I'll be in touch. Be thinking about . . ." He glanced at Enid and Ginger. "You know, what we talked about."

Jack looked nervous as he smiled at Enid and replied to the man. "Sure, I'll do that. Good talking with you."

Ginger glanced at Enid and then at Jack as he walked backed to his office. "Something's up."

CHAPTER 10

Enid wanted to follow Jack back to his office and confront him but decided against it. If it was anything she needed to know, he would tell her later. She turned to Ginger. "I'm going to Sarah's to get some tea. Want me to bring anything back for you?"

"Nah, I'm good." She held up a blue and white Red Bull can. At least the energy drink explained some of Ginger's sometimes overly animated behavior.

"Call my cell if you need me."

Enid walked down the street to Sarah's Tea Shoppe, which the locals called Sarah's diner. Only a newcomer would call it a tea shop. In the morning, the place resembled any other small-town diner, catering to businesspeople who commuted to Columbia, as well as retired farmers, and widows and widowers looking for companionship. At lunch, it was a meat-and-three diner, but late afternoon, it transformed into what Sarah had envisioned: a tea shop for Madden's ladies, complete with linen napkins, tiered plates of sweets and small sandwiches, and one of the best selection of teas within fifty miles.

When Enid walked into Sarah's, nearly all of the seats were occupied. As she walked to the counter to put in her to-go order, she heard someone call her name. "Miss Blackwell." And then, "Over here."

She looked to the right side of the small dining area and

saw a man waving at her. She didn't recognize him, but she was well-known in Madden and the surrounding areas because of a series of investigative articles she had written during the past few years. Enid didn't want to talk to anyone until she had her tea, but she also didn't want to be rude, so she walked over to his table.

"I'm sorry, but I don't recall your name," she said.

"Well, that's because we've never met, officially that is. But I read all your articles. You're quite famous around here."

"As they say, I'm a big fish in a small pond."

The man pulled out a chair. "Here, I'd be honored if you would join me."

Enid forced a smile. "I need to get back to the office, but I'll sit for a minute." She instantly regretted her decision. Small talk wasn't her best skill. At times like this, she wished she wasn't such an introvert who valued her privacy. She envied women who could chat away about nothing with ease. "I don't recall seeing you here before," she said. "You must work at the distribution center."

"Well, I do a little contract work for them now and then. I'm in IT. You know, computers and networks."

"Do you live in Madden?" Enid thought she detected a slight crack in his cheery smile, but he quickly recovered.

"Now I know what it feels like to be interviewed by you."

"I'm sorry, I didn't mean to interrogate you, it's just that . . ." She stood up. "Anyway, I need to get back to the office. Take care." She rushed away before he could object.

When Enid got back to the office, she realized she had never gotten her tea, so she rummaged around in her desk and found an old tea bag. One corner had torn, and half the leaves were in her drawer. In frustration, she slammed her drawer shut.

"Maybe I should come back later."

Enid jumped when she heard Jack's voice. "Sorry. Do you need something?"

"We can talk later. Seriously."

"Is this about your visitor?"

Jack blushed slightly. "Yes, but it can wait."

"I desperately need a cup of tea. Then we can talk."

"I think we've got some Earl Grey in the breakroom. Come on, I'll buy you a cup."

Enid followed Jack to the small area at the end of the hall they jokingly referred to as the office breakroom. But it was only a small wooden table with an oilcloth covering and a coffeemaker, a bowl of sugar, a container of powdered creamer, and a couple packets of Splenda alongside a small electric tea kettle.

Jack pulled up the table covering and reached into the small drawer beneath, rummaging his hand around since he couldn't see inside. "Ah, here we go." He pulled out a couple of tea bags. "Earl Grey, your favorite."

Enid took the tea bags from him. "How long have these been in the drawer?"

"Well, they can't be more than several years old. I think I bought them when you first came to work here." He held them out to Enid.

"Thanks, but I think I'll pass."

Jack shrugged. "Okay, suit yourself. Sure you won't take a cup of coffee instead?"

Enid shook her head. "No, I'm good."

Jack motioned toward his office with his arm. "After you, madam."

Enid walked in and moved a stack of files off the chair

across from Jack's desk. "Should I let Ginger file these back for you?"

Jack reached for the files and cleared his throat. "No, these are private files."

Enid glanced at the label on the top file, "Financial Reports," and then handed them to Jack.

Jack settled into his chair and Enid waited for him to speak first. He rubbed his neck, a tell that he was anxious or stressed. "I really don't know where to start," he said.

Enid waited for him to find his words.

"It's been a tough couple of years, not just for the *Tri-County Gazette*, but for journalism in general. The shift to digital has made print advertisers skittish, and people are turning to other sources for the news, which means revenue dropped substantially."

Enid smiled. "Facebook, Twitter, TicTok. Those are hardly reliable news sources, but I know what you mean."

"Last year, newsroom layoffs here in the US reached a record high, growing nearly two hundred percent compared to last year. And in the last fifteen years, more than a quarter of the country's print newspapers closed, leaving many rural residents without local news. I don't want that to happen here, but I won't lie. Times are tough."

Enid took a deep breath. "So are you laying me off? Or firing me?"

Jack slapped the desk with his palms. "Goodness, no." He paused. "Nearly a year of cancer treatment took a lot out of me, physically and mentally. I just don't have the same drive to keep fighting what might be the inevitable." He sighed. "I may sell the paper."

CHAPTER 11

Enid sat across from Jack staring at him, hoping he would laugh and say he was kidding. Except he wasn't. "I'm not sure what to say. When will this happen?" She had a million other questions, but they could wait until later. "That man, your friend from Chicago, is he the buyer?"

"We're just talking at this point. He contacted me out of the blue and asked if I was willing to sell. He wants me to put a price on the *Tri-County Gazette*."

"But this is your life. What will you do? Move somewhere and go to work for a big paper again?"

"No, I won't go back into the big newspaper rat race. They want young kids who'll work for a dime until they move for better pay or into another field. Besides, I'm ready to do something different."

"Sounds like you've made up your mind."

"Let's just say I'm considering it. It's you I'm worried about."

"I can't say this is not a shock, because it is. But one thing I've learned since my divorce is not to take anything for granted. The change might be good for me too. But what I'll miss the most are the people here."

"Whoa, let's not pack our bags yet. I haven't signed anything." He paused. "Would you really leave Madden?"

"I haven't had time to think it through obviously, but there's nothing for me here other than you and the friends

I've made. What would I do in Madden if the paper is bought out? And what about Josh? He joked that if he came back here, he'd have to drive a forklift at the distribution center."

"I know you miss Josh. I do too. Hopefully, he'll return from New Mexico soon and you two can figure out your relationship. Until then, you can work for the new owner. He's already asked me if you'd stay. And I've still got good contacts at other papers I can connect you with. I'm sure any paper will want you. In fact, I get questions all the time about why you haven't moved on."

"Well, don't worry about me. I'm not sure what I'll do. When I came here to work for you, I thought being a reporter was what I wanted. But Josh's leaving changed my outlook on life. My work is less important now than it once was, so I'm not so sure about anything now." Enid held up her hand. "Oh, I almost forgot. Cade called from London."

"Oh, great. How's he doing?"

"He's getting married."

Jack leaned back in his chair. "I can't say I'm shocked. Do you know her?"

Enid shook her head. "She's British, owns a boutique in London."

"At the risk of sounding like an armchair psychologist, how do you feel about it?"

"Like you, I'm not shocked. I'm happy for him. Cade and I were once great together, but things changed." Enid glanced at the big schoolroom-style clock on Jack's wall. "I need to get a few things done. Thanks for confiding in me. I won't tell anyone, although I think Ginger already has her suspicions."

Jack smiled. "She would. You know, she's really a lot

smarter than I've given her credit for."

"She's good at research too. I hope you'll help her find something if you sell the paper."

"Of course. I'll help her any way I can."

Enid's cell phone vibrated in her jacket pocket as she stood up. "I've got a call," she said as she left Jack's office. She glanced at the screen: "Joe Kerr" was the caller.

"Hello."

The now familiar altered voice said: "Hello, Enid. This is your friend Joe. Do you have a minute to talk?"

Enid rushed into her office and shut the door. "Who are you and why are you calling me? This has to stop."

"But why? I'm a big fan, so I wouldn't hurt you. I just want you to be recognized for the great reporter you are. Now, is that so bad of me?"

"Thanks, but I don't need your help. Now stop calling me." She tapped the red button and cut him off. Immediately, her phone rang again. It was Ty, the *State* newspaper reporter. "What?" she answered.

"Having a bad day, are we?" Ty asked.

Enid rubbed her pounding temple with her free hand. "Sorry. Yes, it is a bit of a bad day. What can I help you with?"

"I'm headed up your way now. Can we sit down and talk?"

"About what? You've obviously got your sources, so I doubt I can help you. Besides, I told you no earlier."

"Just a cup of coffee at that place . . . can't remember the name."

"Unless you want a cup of coffee from the Exxon station snack bar, you must mean Sarah's."

"That's it. See you there in about fifteen." He hung up

before Enid could reply.

CHAPTER 12

As Enid walked into Sarah's diner, she realized she didn't know what Ty looked like. He sounded young, and she guessed he would stand out like a sore thumb, maybe because he was so irritating. She glanced around for anyone who looked out of place, but with the new people in town, there were several people who fit that description. When she felt the tap on her shoulder, she nearly fell over as she whirled around to face the man behind her.

"Sorry, didn't mean to startle you," he said, holding out his hand. "I'm Ty."

Enid ignored his outstretched hand. "You really know how to be irritating, don't you." He was as young as he sounded.

He laughed. "What? They didn't teach you 'How to Be Annoying 101' when you studied journalism?" Without waiting for her reply, he motioned to an open table. "Come on, let's sit. I promise not to keep you long."

When the waitperson arrived at their table, she spoke to Enid first. "Like your cup of Earl Grey?"

"Yes, that would be nice."

Ty looked at their waitperson's nameplate and smiled. "And, Jackie, I'll have a cup of coffee. I'm assuming you don't have a Chi Latte here in Madden."

"Why, gosh," Jackie said with an exaggerated Southern accent. "I don't suppose I rightly know what that is." She winked at Enid. "But if you'd like one, we can surely find out and whip it up for you."

Ty blushed slightly. "That would be nice. Thanks." He waited for Jackie to leave and then said to Enid, "They don't like outsiders here, I see."

"We only dislike outsiders who assume we're from the backwoods. Besides, Jackie enjoys having someone to dish it out to, considering how much she has to take herself."

Jackie brought their drinks and looked at Ty. "I'll check back on y'all later to see if you need anything. Miss Enid is one of my favorites."

Ty sipped his drink. "That's actually pretty good." And then he quickly added, "For anywhere, not just Madden."

Enid glanced at the time on her phone. "I really don't have long. Can you tell me what this is all about?"

"Fair enough. I promised to be brief. I think the person who took Mia and Winnie is fixated on you."

"Based on what? One irresponsible comment by your 'source'?"

"Have you heard from him again?"

"Are we on the record or off?" Enid asked.

Ty shrugged. "Whatever you want."

"I want you to go away and leave me alone, but that's unlikely."

"Thanks. For a newsman, that's a compliment."

In spite of herself, Enid smiled. "That's what Cade would have said."

"He your husband or boyfriend?"

"My ex."

"I see. Well, we can talk off the record. After all, I realize you don't know me."

"How long have you been with the *State*?"

"Not long. I came here less than a year ago. I was a reporter in New Mexico for a while, but I missed green grass, so I came back South."

Enid felt a shiver when he mentioned New Mexico. She reminded herself that New Mexico is a big state, so she decided not to ask him anything further about it or if he knew Josh. Besides, she didn't want to prolong the conversation any longer than necessary.

"So," Ty said, "have you heard from this guy again?"

"I'm not sure this isn't all just a prank. His name on my phone screen is Joe Kerr."

"You mean like joker?"

"Exactly."

"Well, at least your caller is clever."

"What is it exactly that you want from me? You and the other daily reporters will be all over this one, and you don't need my help."

"On the contrary, you've done some amazing reporting, especially for a weekly reporter."

"Don't be condescending, Ty."

"Twice in one day would be a crime, I suppose." He smiled, showing nearly perfect white teeth. "I want to team up with you to report on this. You see, having a local, highly respected journalist would give me the edge over my competition."

Enid glanced at the time again. "I'll consider your overwhelming offer, but don't call me, I'll call you." She stood to leave. "You can get the bill. And leave Jackie a nice tip. Then she might overlook your lack of sensitivity."

CHAPTER 13

When Enid returned to the newspaper office, she stopped at Ginger's desk. "Do you have time to help me with something?"

"Sure. What's up?"

"I'd like to know more about a *State* newspaper reporter named Ty."

"Last name?" Ginger asked.

"I don't remember if he told me, but he should be easy to find. I'd like to know how long he's worked there, his previous employers, and whatever else you can find out."

Ginger's left eyebrow raised. "Giving up on Josh coming back?"

"What? No, nothing like that. This guy Ty wants to work with me on Winifred Tucker's disappearance. He thinks Mia's disappearance is related."

"We've been getting calls all morning about Mia," Ginger said. "I guess the word is out that she's missing." She leaned in toward Enid and whispered. "And that guy that was here is trying to reach Jack." She frowned. "I was kinda hoping . . ."

"Hoping for what?"

"You know, that maybe I could study with you and Jack and do a few articles here and there. You know, just the ones you didn't want."

"Ginger, are you saying you want to be a reporter?"

"Well, you know, it's just a fantasy. I can't afford to go to journalism school. But I do have a degree in English, not that it's helped me a lot."

"Have you talked to Jack about this?"

"I've been putting it off. And now, well, you know. I kinda overheard part of their conversation. That guy wants to buy the paper." She paused. "But Jack wouldn't sell, would he?"

"Jack's had a rough go of it. His cancer is in remission, but I'm sure he'd like to enjoy life a bit more. I can't blame him. Newspapers are dying, so I'm afraid you might find out you're stepping into a field that won't exist much longer, at least as we know it. But I'll be happy to talk to Jack for you once we know what's going on."

"Great. So I'll see what I can find out about this guy Ty." When Enid began walking away, Ginger called out, "What about that good looking man of yours? When is Josh coming home?"

"He is home, in New Mexico. This is not home for him." She walked back to her office and sat at her desk. For a moment she closed her eyes and tried to visualize what life would be like for her if Jack did sell the paper. What would she do? Where would she go? Was Josh even part of her plans any longer?

Her thoughts were interrupted by Ginger. "I've got something on your guy Ty."

"That was quick."

"Are you ready for this?" Without waiting for a reply, Ginger continued. "Well, our guy Ty is quite the celeb. He won a couple of awards while working for other newspapers, but he's got a reputation for being out for himself. Not that that's bad, of course."

"Wait." Enid interrupted her. "How do you know this?"

"Well, you see, my roommate dates a guy that works, or well he did work, at the *State*, and—"

"Never mind, just go on."

"Well, like I said, he's known for being very aggressive, to the point of being obnoxious."

"I can vouch for that," Enid said. "But is he legit?"

"Far as I can tell. I've printed out some of his articles for you. He's pretty good, actually. What else do you want to know about him?"

"Nothing else for now. Thanks for jumping right on that."

"Sure thing." She stood to leave. "Oh, by the way, some guy dropped off a package for you a few minutes ago. I'll go get it."

"What guy? UPS or the mailman?"

"Sorry. I didn't see him leave it. It was on my desk. I'll get it for you."

When Ginger returned with the package, she laid it on Enid's desk. "Here you go. Just let me know if you need anything else. Except cleaning your house. I'm not that desperate for you to help me."

Enid laughed. The old Ginger was back. Enid actually preferred her straightforward, no nonsense demeanor. At least you never had to guess where you stood with her.

The package was about ten by twelve inches and addressed to Enid Blackwell, no address, so it didn't come through the mail. No return name or address. She started to open it, but stopped. She took her pen and pushed the package to get an idea of how heavy it was. Something shifted inside.

She left the package on her desk and walked to Jack's

office. His door was open. "Can I run something past you?"

He pulled his half-rim glasses off and put them on his desk. "Sure. Come on in."

Enid sat in the metal chair across from his desk. "I'm not sure, that is, I don't want to bother you with something that's probably nothing, but . . ."

"You're never a bother, now spit it out. What's going on?"

"I've got a package delivered to me. I haven't opened it because I'm afraid it's from Joe Kerr, although I'm sure that's not his real name, because if you say it fast it sounds like joker."

Jack held up his hand. "Whoa. I have no idea what you're talking about."

"Sorry. I guess I'm a little rattled."

"That's not like you. You've gotten yourself in some pretty serious situations, and I've rarely seen you rattled."

"This might be about Mia. And Winnie. But I'm not sure."

"What was in the package?" Jack asked.

"I haven't opened it. I was wondering if I should take it to Pete at the police station."

"This is starting to sound serious. Let's go look at it."

Jack and Enid walked back to her office. The cardboard box that looked so ominous earlier was now just a box. "I feel silly," she said.

"Well, don't." Jack put his glasses on. "No return, no name. How'd it get here?"

"Ginger said someone dropped it off."

"Do you think it was Joker?"

"I didn't say his name was Joker. I just said Joe Kerr sounds like joker. Joe Kerr might really be his name."

"And how do you know him?"

"I think he's probably the same guy I told you about who's been calling me."

"Here at the office?"

"No, on my personal cell phone. I don't know how he got the number. I called back and it's not a working number."

"And what did he say when he called you?"

"He said he wanted to make me famous, so I'd get the recognition I deserved."

"How many times has he called you?"

"A couple times."

Jack picked up her office phone and punched in a number. "Pete, this is Jack. Can you come over to the newspaper office right away? It's urgent."

CHAPTER 14

Pete Barnes was the youngest police chief in Madden's history. He wasn't the most experienced lawman, but he did have the attributes most wanted in a small-town police chief. He was personable, and he ate and enjoyed all the food the town ladies brought him. More importantly, he was good with technology and often worked on the mayor's business and personal computers. Last week, he programmed a universal remote at her house, which would likely ensure the mayor's continued endorsement of the police chief.

Pete's mentor was Joshua Hart, the former Madden police chief and Bowman County sheriff. Josh was instrumental in Pete's promotion when Josh left the position to become the county sheriff. In many ways, Pete idolized his mentor, although Pete had no aspirations of being promoted to sheriff or moving to a bigger town. He was happiest when working on computers or flying his drone out in an open field. Once, he piloted the drone around town, but after his office got inundated with calls about spies, he began surveying the rural areas instead with the drone's onboard camera.

Madden was mostly a peaceful town, although the influx of newcomers in and around it had brought new, mostly petty crimes to the area. When Pete got the call from Jack, he was concerned because it was from Jack. The police station often got crazy calls and complaints from other citizens, but not from Jack. If he felt it warranted calling, then Pete knew it was important.

He walked briskly down Madden's main street to the newspaper office, only a few buildings away. Ginger was waiting for him and escorted him back to Enid's office, where she and Jack were staring at the box.

"Hi, Pete," Jack said. "Thanks for coming."

"Sure thing." Pete glanced at the box. "What's going on?"

Enid spoke first. "Why don't you sit down and let me fill you in." Jack pulled another chair from his office, and Jack and Pete sat across from Enid at her desk.

Enid told Pete about her calls from Joe Kerr and about Ty's insistence to be involved. "Then this arrived today, hand delivered here."

Pete stood over the package and looked at it from all angles. "I think I need to call SLED, since they're taking the lead on Mia and Winifred's disappearances. Bowman County has never handled anything like this. Plus, this is the second mysterious package you've gotten, and if this one has anything to do with Winifred Tucker or Mia, they need to know."

"I'm going to feel foolish if it turns out to be something silly, like free tickets to the fall festival," Enid said. "But this whole thing has me spooked."

"You know, reporters being harassed and stalked has become a big problem," Jack said. "You are right to be careful."

Pete nodded and called SLED from his cell phone. "They're sending out a bomb squad now. In the meantime, we need to evacuate all of you."

"Pete, we've been standing around looking at it for nearly

half an hour. If we don't touch it, why do we have to evacuate? It'll take SLED at least another thirty minutes to get here."

"Actually, they have an agent at the Tucker house now, so he'll be here shortly." He motioned for them to go outside. "Come on, let's just be smart about this."

When the South Carolina Law Enforcement officer arrived, he introduced himself and instructed everyone to step away from the building. He asked where the package was and went inside alone. A few minutes later, he told Jack the bomb squad would take it away, as he pointed to the big black truck driving up.

Ginger was busy taking notes, while Jack, Pete, and Enid watched SLED put the enshrouded box into the truck and drive away. The SLED officer told Jack they would let him know what was going on once they examined the box. For now, there was nothing else to be done.

"Before I leave," Pete said to Enid, "can I ask you a few questions?"

"Sure, do you want me to come to the police station?"

"No, here is fine."

"We can go to my office."

Pete followed Enid down the hallway and into her small office. "According to Mrs. Tucker, before she went missing, Mia talked to the stable manager at the Tucker farm, just like Winifred Tucker talked to Chad just before she vanished. I think his name was Brad. No wait, Chad. Did Mia mention him to you at all?"

"No, I don't recall her saying anything about him. Why?"

Pete hesitated. "Can we be off the record?"

Enid looked puzzled. "Sure."

"He's gone AWOL."

"He quit?"

"Mrs. Tucker told me Chad fed the horses last night, but this morning, he's gone. He must have left during the night. He took all his belongings with him."

"Three people are now missing, and they all seem to be connected."

Pete nodded. "Yep. If you get any more calls from that Joe Kerr fella, let me know right away." As he started to leave, he turned back to Enid. "I miss Josh."

"Me too."

CHAPTER 15

Ginger ran into Enid's office. "I've got great notes about all this if you need them."

"We can't do an article on this. Not until we know what's going on. Unfortunately, we're not objective reporters now. We are the news." Enid couldn't believe she was quoting Ty.

Ginger looked disappointed. "Well, maybe later."

"Hold on to those notes, and we'll see if Jack will let you do an article later."

Ginger beamed and strutted back to her desk.

Ty's words weren't the only ones stuck in Enid's head. She also thought of Pete's: "I miss Josh." She had promised herself she would not reach out to him while he was gone. He reunited with his sister Heather and was staying with her in New Mexico. He had called once or twice, but they both agreed they needed space to figure out their futures. After Josh quit his gang task force job with the governor's office, he was unemployed. He had used up his good graces with Governor Larkin, and it was unlikely he could get another sheriff's position in the state. Josh and Enid also had to work out their conflicts of interest. Their paths crossed frequently as she reported on crime in the tri-county area, creating suspicion and accusations of unfair access and confidentiality breaches, none of which were true. They worked hard to keep their work separated, but rumors can't be controlled.

Pushing her promise aside, she picked up the phone to call Josh. And stopped herself. What would she say? And what would happen if he agreed to come back to South Carolina? As she rubbed her throbbing temples, her office phone rang. Ty's number showed on the screen. She didn't want to talk to him, so she ignored it. Hopefully, Ginger would pick up the call at her desk. But it kept ringing.

"Hello, Ty." She tried not to let her dread show in her voice.

"Hello, Ms. Blackwell, or did we agree I could call you Enid?"

"Enid is fine. What do you need?"

"I heard about your package."

Enid's shoulders stiffened. "How did you know about that?"

"I told you I have my sources."

Who could have told him? Certainly not Jack or Pete. "I can't talk to you. This is an ongoing investigation, and I promised Police Chief Barnes I wouldn't use any of it for a story. Not yet, anyway."

"But you won't. I will. See, that's what makes our collaboration work so well."

"We're not collaborating. You're asking me to do something unethical, and I won't be a part of your little scheme. Besides, if you have such great sources, you don't need me. I've got to go. Goodbye." Enid's hands were trembling, and she was irritated with Ginger for not answering the phone. Enid marched to the front of the office to confront Ginger, but she wasn't at her desk. Just as well. Taking out her frustrations on Ginger wasn't fair.

Enid walked back to the office to get her tote and to tell Jack she was going to work from home. The newspaper office used to be her sanctuary. But not now. She put a few files and her laptop in her tote and scooped up a few phone messages from earlier in the day. Grabbing her cell phone, she walked down the hall to tell Jack she was leaving, but his office door was closed. She heard a man's voice—likely his friend from Chicago, the potential buyer. Enid texted Jack and told him to call her at home if he needed anything.

The drive to her small bungalow just outside of Madden was only a few minutes away from town, but it was a bit isolated. She rented it from one of Jack's friends. He offered to sell it to her, and she was tempted. But now, if the paper was sold, she might not have a future in Madden.

Rarely did she feel lonely, even though she lived alone. But this afternoon she needed a friend. *I miss Josh.*

CHAPTER 16

When Enid walked into her home, she turned on the lights, kicked her shoes off, and threw her tote on the floor beside the small desk in her spare bedroom. Work could wait. What she needed was a hot shower and a cup of tea. Or maybe even a glass of red wine. Her spirits were rising a bit when she heard her cell phone ringing. She dug down into the bottom of her tote and grabbed it without looking at the screen, assuming it was probably Jack. "Hello?"

"Hello, beautiful."

"Who is this?" Enid stiffened.

"Did you like my present?"

"What do you want from me?"

"I know you want to enjoy your time at home, so I'll let you go. For now." The call ended.

Enid had been holding her breath and exhaled deeply after he hung up. Her hands were trembling. She quickly checked the doors to be sure they were locked. She looked out the window of her bedroom, which faced the woods behind her house. After a minute or so, she was comfortable no one was watching, or at least she didn't see any movement.

Sitting on the side of the bed, she put her face in her hands. "Why me?" she said aloud. She didn't want to alarm Jack, but she needed to let someone know. Maybe she should call Pete. She jumped when her cell phone rang again. This time the screen confirmed it was Jack. "I'm so glad you called."

"Well, that's nice of you to say so. Are you alright?"

"I . . . Could you come over when you leave the office? I just need someone to talk to."

"I would love to, but I'm having dinner with my friend from Chicago."

"The potential buyer. That's fine. We'll do it some other time. Did you need something?"

"I just wanted to tell you SLED said your box wasn't a bomb or anything dangerous."

"Well, there's some good news finally. So what was it?"

"They didn't say exactly, but the SLED agent asked if Mia used a Portage reporter's notebook."

Enid felt the air leaving her lungs. "She did."

"I know," Jack said. "That's all they would tell me."

"What's happening? Why am I being targeted?"

"I'm afraid you've got yourself a stalker, and I'm worried about you. Your room at my house is still available. Why not come here until all this is over?"

"I'm not going to let some maniac run me out of my house." But even as she said it, she was challenging herself to be logical.

"Do you still have the 9mm Josh bought you? I bet you haven't been to the shooting range in a while."

"Yes, I have it in the small chest beside my bed."

"Make sure it's loaded. See you in the morning then?"

"Sure."

As Jack suggested, Enid checked the bedside chest to be sure the gun was loaded and the safety on. The cold metal in her hand made her shiver. As much as she hated violence, guns were a necessary evil these days, especially for women living alone. She pulled her concealed carry permit from the drawer and put it in her tote.

Tomorrow, after her meeting with Jack and the SLED agent, she planned to call T-Mobile and get them to assign her a new number. She fell asleep mentally listing the people she would need to notify.

• • •

He parked his car on the street so as not to awaken his beloved Enid Blackwell. Then he quietly walked up the long dirt driveway to her house. A porch light illuminated the area. He glanced around. The nearest house was hidden beyond a tall stand of pine trees gently swaying in the breeze.

Walking up to the porch, he smiled to himself. Oh how he wished he could be there to see her face when she opened his present. He laid the small box at her doorstep and quietly returned to his car, thinking about how much he loved Enid Blackwell. Maybe one day she would love him too.

CHAPTER 17

After a slow start the next morning, Enid rushed to get ready. She had tossed all night, unable to put the phone calls and package delivered to her office out of her mind. She grabbed her tote and headed out the door.

When her foot hit the small white box, she nearly tripped. It was about the size of a manuscript box, with no address or markings on it. Maybe Jack or Ginger had dropped something off for her to review. It wasn't there when she came home, but it could have been dropped off later and they decided not to disturb her.

She picked the box up and felt something shift inside. Whatever it was, it was light. Since she was running late, her first instinct was to throw the box in the car and open it at the office. But whoever left it had intended for her to see it first thing. Maybe it was something Jack needed her to review right away.

She sat on the painted rocker on her small porch and opened the box. Inside was a small bracelet of pink braided leather. A lone silver charm hung from it, and something was engraved on it. Enid examined it closer. Her heart beat rapidly as she read the one-word inscription: Winnie.

"Oh, no." Admonishing herself to remain calm, she called the Madden police station. "Pete, I just got something else from my stalker. It was left on my porch during the night apparently, and it seems to be Winnie's bracelet. At least it has her name on it."

"Where are you now?"

"I'm still here, at my house, on the porch."

"Go inside and lock the door. I'll send a deputy out and then we'll contact SLED."

Enid glanced around and then backed into her house, putting the deadbolt on the door. She laid the package on her dining table.

A few minutes later, a Madden police car pulled into her driveway, and a tall, muscular deputy walked toward the house. Enid opened the door when she recognized him as one of the deputies she had seen around town.

"Good morning, ma'am," he said. "Police Chief Barnes asked me to wait here until SLED picks up the package. I'll just be out in the car."

"You're welcome to wait inside."

"No, ma'am, but thanks. I'll just be outside. I might walk around a bit and see if I see anything." He handed her a business card. "Here's my cell number in case you need me. Don't go outside."

After the deputy left, Enid called Jack and filled him in on what had happened."

"You should have come to my house. Your house is too isolated for you to stay there alone. Once you've talked to SLED, I'm coming to get you."

"I know you're concerned, but we can discuss this later." Just as she ended the call, another call came through on her cell phone. This time, she recognized the name but was afraid it was another prank from her tormentor. "Hello."

"Are you missing me as much as I miss you?"

"Josh, is that really you?" She wanted to cry with relief. The stress of the past week was wearing her down and making her unusually emotional. "How did you know how much I needed to talk to you?" Before he could reply, she added. "Wait. Which one of them called you? Pete or Jack?"

"Actually, they both did. And before you get all indignant about them being overly protective, remember they both care about you and are worried. And they both know how hardheaded you can be about not wanting anyone to help you."

Josh was right. Her instant reaction was irritation with Jack and Pete. But for now, she was just happy to talk to Josh. "I guess they told you what's going on here."

"They did. Do you have any idea who this stalker is?"

"None whatsoever."

Josh and Enid started to speak at the same time and then laughed together. "You first," Josh said.

"I wanted to call you, but I knew you needed space."

"That's exactly what I was going to say to you. We've put ourselves in a fine mess here, haven't we." He paused. "I've got a few things to finish here. I'm helping my sister fix up a small house she bought. After that, if you're okay with it, I'd like to come back and visit with you. We need to talk."

"I'd love to see you again."

"In the meantime, Jack said he's invited you to stay with him. I think you should."

"I don't want to leave my house, but I'll consider it. Did Jack tell you about what's going on with the paper?"

"No, he didn't mention anything. What's happening?"

"I'll fill you in later. I just saw another car drive up. It might be the SLED agent."

"Pete says it appears the young girl and your reporter were both abducted. Please be careful. He's obviously got you in his sights now, and I don't know what I'd do if something happened to you. Promise me you'll accept protection and watch your back."

"I will. I promise. I've got to go now."

CHAPTER 18

After talking with Josh, Enid looked out the front window and saw the deputy talking with another familiar face: Ty, the *State* newspaper reporter. *Oh, great. Just what I need.*

The deputy walked up to the door and Enid opened it before he knocked. "Ma'am, do you know this man? He says you wanted to see him."

"Well, that's certainly not true, but I do know him."

"Do you want to see him?"

Enid was tempted to send Ty away, but agreed to meet with him on the porch. She didn't want him eyeing the package on her table. But if he really did have the sources he claimed, then he already knew about it.

"I'll keep an eye on him from the car."

"Oh, he's not the stalker, he's just an annoying reporter." Enid smiled to herself. *Did I really just say that?*

The deputy motioned for Ty to come up to the porch. "Stay right here where I can see you."

Enid sat in one of the rockers. "You can sit for a minute if you want to." She waited for Ty to settle in. "Why are you here?"

"I've got something I want you to hear." Ty pulled his cell phone from his pocket and tapped play on a recording.

The same altered voice that had been calling Enid spoke:

"I want you to tell my story. About how I fell in love with Enid Blackwell, and then how I made her famous. Ask her if she likes the presents I sent her."

Then Ty's voice: "What do you want out of all this? Recognition? Thanks from Ms. Blackwell?"

A disembodied laugh followed, making her shiver: "I want her to be mine forever."

"Turn it off," Enid said. "I don't want to hear this crazy talk. You need to take that to the police."

"I will, but I wanted you to hear it first. You know, professional courtesy between reporters. I assume he was referring to Mia's notebook he sent to you."

How did Ty know about that? "I'm sure there's more to your visit than chumming up to me. What do you want? An exclusive, I assume."

"There's no shame in asking. You should understand. I'm just doing my job. Besides, SLED will be monitoring all of your conversations so you won't be able to have any communication with this guy, not privately at least. If we leave my communication line to him open, we might be able to find out something that will help catch him."

"I'm not going to be a part of any scheme that undermines the authorities. And frankly, I don't want to stay in touch with that creep." Enid stood. "I think you should leave now. I'm going to tell SLED about your phone call, so you might want to tell them first."

"Alright, have it your way. But I think you're missing out on an opportunity to stay in touch with this guy. If they tap my phone, which they surely will, we have no way for him to contact us, and then he's likely to take someone else in frustration. Is that what you want?"

"Don't try to pin this guy's actions on me by trying to manipulate me. And you're assuming SLED and the local authorities can't capture him. I'm much more optimistic than you are. Let's let them do their jobs."

Before Ty could respond, a black SUV drove up. "I guess they want to take a look at your latest present."

"You need to stay and talk to them about the phone call," Enid said.

"You tell them if you want to, but I'm leaving." Ty took long strides toward his car, nodding at the deputy sheriff as he passed him.

The SLED agent introduced himself to Enid and then followed her inside. She pointed to the box on her dining table. "There. That's it."

"You've opened it?"

"I had no idea it was from the stalker. I thought it was from my office." She felt stupid as she said it out loud.

The agent put on gloves and carried the box outside. "Wait here. I'll be back."

When the agent returned, he asked her to sit. "We need to get the local police to put you under surveillance. But we want to keep it as inconspicuous as possible. If he's brave enough to come to your house, we'd like for him to do it again. Of course, we'll be nearby to grab him."

"I doubt he's that stupid. And I need to tell you about the stalker's contact with another reporter."

The SLED agent's eyebrow cocked up on one side. "Excuse me?"

Enid told him about Ty and the latest phone call he had received. "I tried to get him to stay and talk with you."

The agent's jaw tightened. "Give me all you know about this reporter, his phone number, email, anything you've got."

Enid wrote down Ty's phone and email on a slip of paper. "That's all I have. He works for the *State* newspaper.

I'm sure you can find him there."

CHAPTER 19

After the SLED agent left, Enid showered and dressed for the office. When she opened her front door to leave, the deputy sheriff approached her. "Ma'am, you need to stay inside."

"I am not going to be a prisoner in my own home. If you want to arrest me, then go ahead. Otherwise, you can follow me to work if you want to." She walked to her car in the driveway and backed around so that she was driving forward to the secondary road that would take her into town. When she glanced in the rearview mirror, the deputy was behind her, talking into the police radio mike on his shoulder.

When she walked into the newspaper office, Jack was at Ginger's desk. "I didn't expect you to come in." He glanced out the window. "I see you've got company."

Without responding, Enid marched to her office and slammed the door.

She didn't owe Ty a heads up, but like he said, it was professional courtesy. She called his cell number. No answer. She tried to text him, and after no response, she called his office. After a few rings, his answering service kicked in. "Ty, this is Enid. Call me now. I'm not in the mood to play games."

She went to the small break area to make a cup of tea with the fresh tea bags she brought from home. When she walked by Jack's office, he was sitting at his desk, staring off into space. She tapped on his open door. "Got a minute?"

At the sound of her voice, Jack looked toward her. "Oh, sorry. Sure, come on in."

She sat in the chair across from him. "I'm sorry for behaving the way I did earlier. This whole mess has got me rattled. I hope they catch him soon so my life can get back to some kind of normal again."

Jack nodded. "I know, and I'm so sorry you're going through all this." He paused. "I don't want to add to your stress, but I don't want you to hear this from anyone but me."

Enid's hand flew to her mouth. "Oh, no. Has your cancer returned?"

"No, nothing that serious. It's just that—"

"You've sold the paper."

"It's beginning to look that way. We're getting pretty serious. Darren Smoak, my friend from Chicago, really wants to buy it. And, quite honestly, I'm tired. I want to fly fish in mountain streams, cook real food again, and not worry constantly about deadlines."

"I understand."

"Darren wants to talk with you. He wants you to stay, of course."

"I'm not going to make that commitment. Not now. But I'll be glad to talk to him."

"Thanks. You won't get any interference from me, one way or the other."

"What kind of person is Darren? I suppose, if you're long-time friends, he must be an okay guy."

"We were not close friends, just acquaintances. He's younger than me, and I mentored him. For a short time, at least."

"But he left the newspaper business."

Jack laughed. "Guess that doesn't say much for my mentoring. Darren's family is wealthy, and he returned to the family business for a while. Now he wants to buy a local paper and get back into it."

"Does he understand the challenges of a small-town, weekly paper?"

"Oddly enough, he does. I'm impressed with the research he's done. And actually, many small papers are doing better than the big ones. People go online for the national news, but they still rely on papers like the *Tri-County Gazette* for their local news."

"But you said the paper was struggling financially."

"We're holding our own for now and doing better than most, but we have no cushion for expansion, upgrades, or emergencies. Unless I tap into personal funds."

"Like I said, I'll be happy to talk with him, but I'm not sure what I'll do. Oh, by the way, Josh called. I should be mad at you and Pete for calling him, but it was really good to hear his voice."

Jack leaned back in his chair. "Is he coming back?"

Enid shrugged. "He said he is, but he didn't say when or for how long. We'll just have to play it by ear."

Ginger tapped on the door. "We've got a lot of calls coming in from other newspapers. Everyone wants to talk to you. Both of you, actually."

"Thanks. I'll handle it," Jack said.

After Ginger left, Jack said, "For now, don't discuss Darren with Ginger, although she's probably figured it all out. As for the other reporters wanting to know about Mia, continue to run everything through me."

"Before I go, I need to tell you about my conversation

with Ty."

After Enid filled Jack in on the stalker's call to Ty, he ran his hands through his hair. "Whew. This is getting too close and too scary. You've got to come stay with me."

"SLED wants me to stay at my house, and they're going to watch it in case this creep tries to drop off anything else."

"The only good thing about this mess is that it's making my decision to sell even easier. There was a time when I would have found all this exciting, but not now." He reached into his desk. "I almost forgot. I bought you this burner phone so you can keep your current cell number for a while. As much as I hate to say it, we need to stay in touch with this creep. If you change your number, he may try even harder to get physically near you."

"You're beginning to sound like Ty, and I'm beginning to feel like bait."

CHAPTER 20

For the next two days, everything was quiet. The stalker didn't call or send anything else. Enid gave her new phone number to only a few people. Every time her old cell phone rang, she jumped. But no calls from the stalker. Enid was sitting at her desk when Ginger burst in.

"I just heard that Ty is missing," Ginger said.

"What? How do you know that?"

"Remember I told you I had an inside track at the *State*. He's officially MIA."

"That's odd. Let me know if you hear anything else."

"Sure thing."

Enid stared at the top of her desk, trying to wrap her mind around this development. She called Ty's cell number again and got his I'm-sorry-I'm-not-available-to-take-your-call-right-now message. She returned to the article she was writing for this week's edition. The local garden club was selling tickets for a tour of homes around Madden. On one hand, it felt strange to be writing about something as mundane as a home tour with all that was going on. Yet it was also a comforting reminder of normalcy. A knock on her door interrupted her thoughts. Assuming it was Ginger again, she kept typing without looking up. "Hold on a minute."

An unknown male voice replied. "Sure, or I can come back later."

Enid looked up and saw Jack's friend Darren. "I'm sorry, please come in. I thought you were Ginger."

"Are you sure? I don't want to interrupt your work. And I should have made an appointment. Jack may have mentioned that I'm a bit impulsive at times."

"It's fine, really. Have a seat. Just move those files over there."

Darren put the stack of file folders on the floor beside the chair. "I suppose Jack has told you I'm interested in buying the paper. And I'm hoping you'll stay on. You have quite a reputation around this area for your investigative reporting, as well as some national recognition." He smiled. "I never knew weekly papers got into that sort of thing."

"You're right. The bigger papers are generally the ones that get the stories. I'm not sure I'd call myself lucky, just happened to be in the right place." She paused. "I am happy to talk with you, but I'm not ready to commit to staying here."

Another broad smile that reminded Enid of the salesman she bought her car from a few years ago. "Fair enough. I'd just like to share my vision with you. It may help you decide."

"Of course. I'd love to hear your plans."

For the next half hour, Darren talked about going fully digital, moving initially to a twice-weekly format, with the idea of going to a daily format down the road. "Once we're digital only, it would be easy to produce a daily edition. Later, of course."

"With all due respect, Mr. Smoak, I—"

"Please, call me Darren."

"With all due respect, Darren, this is not Chicago. Sometimes we have a hard time filling a weekly paper. Many of our readers are older, and they drop in here or call to share news about scholarships, garden parties, weddings, and other local events. I'm afraid if you go digital, the paper will lose many of its older readers who don't own iPads and iPhones. While it might sound old-fashioned to you, that's one of the things I love about Madden and the tri-county area."

"I completely understand. And you're right, we'll lose some of those customers. My target readers will be the new-comers and younger readers who can accept change." Another big smile. "But I sense you don't approve of my plans."

"It's not my place to approve or disapprove. I'm just not sure this area is ready for your vision. And I'm not sure if I want to be a part of it. But I'll give it some thought."

"Fair enough. Before I let you get back to work, I wanted to say I'm sorry about Mia and this fella that's messing with you. Do you have any idea who it could be?"

"Not at all, but from what little I've learned about stalk-ing, more than six million people a year are victims. Sometimes the stalking is domestic, but often it's a stranger who just becomes obsessed and in his or her mind, the stalker fantasizes about a romantic or close relationship with their victim."

"In preparation for my discussions with Jack, I did quite a bit of research on the newspaper industry. Unfortunately, this is one of the most dangerous times in history for jour-nalists. You might not be in a foreign country or in a war zone, but nonetheless, you may be in just as much danger from this nut job who's after you."

Enid laughed. "Is that your attempt to make me feel bet-ter?"

"Sorry, I know it's personal for you. Forgive my insensitivity." He stood. "Just give our conversation some thought. I promise we'll have a good time transforming this paper together."

"Thanks for the offer. I'll consider it."

After Darren left, Enid tried to focus on work, but it was difficult. While she and others kept referring to him as the stalker, he was likely a kidnapper as well. The thought gave her cold chills. To what lengths would this person go to appease his obsession with her? Maybe Ty and Jack had been right: keep the communication line open so he can be caught.

As soon as that thought crossed her mind, her cell phone rang. She didn't recognize the number. "Hello."

"I can't talk long because they're monitoring your calls."

"Ty, is that you? Where are you?"

"Meet me in Columbia tomorrow morning at eight. There'll be enough rush hour traffic that you can blend in. Write these GPS coordinates down." He gave her two sets of numbers: longitude and latitude. "Make sure you're not followed."

"No, Ty, I'm not going to meet you. SLED is looking for you. I told them about your contact with the stalker."

Ty sighed. "I figured as much. You're never going to get into the big time if you keep playing by the rules."

Enid gripped the phone. "What makes you think . . . Never mind. But I'm not coming, so tell me what you want. Now."

The phone went dead. Enid called the number, but it just kept ringing. Should she tell SLED? Or Jack? She picked up her tote and headed toward Ginger's desk. "I'm going to Sarah's for a muffin. Want me to bring you anything?"

"No, I'm good. You alright? You look upset."
"Just need some time to think. I'll be back soon."

CHAPTER 21

Sarah's had the usual assortment of patrons when Enid walked in. She looked at the back table, where she normally sat, but it was occupied. The man sitting there looked up and smiled, motioning for her to join him. Oh, great, it was that guy who called her over once before. She smiled and took another seat over by the window. A young woman came over immediately and took Enid's order. As she turned to leave, she said to Enid in a low voice, "I think you have an admirer." She nodded toward the back table.

"Why do you say that?"

"He asked me if that reporter lady was coming in today."

"I hope you didn't tell him anything about me."

"Oh no, girl. I wouldn't do that to you. Although he's harmless enough. He's in here every day." She laughed. "Lucky me."

Enid pushed her uneasiness aside and pulled out a note pad to capture what she knew so far, making a list.

-Winnie disappears after walking from the horse barn on their property.

- Mia went to see Mrs. Tucker and disappeared soon after.

- Someone sent Mia's reporter notebook to the newspaper office.

- Someone sent Winnie's bracelet to my house.

- Someone claiming to be the stalker contacted Ty at his office.

- Ty has inside information. From whom?

Enid was lost in her thoughts studying the list when a male voice interrupted her.

"Hello, I hope I'm not bothering you." It was the man from the back table.

"Actually, I'm working on something, and I have a deadline."

"Oh, of course. I just wanted to say hello. Maybe we can talk next time."

Enid put her pen down. "I don't mean to be rude, but I'm not interested in bonding with you or whatever this is. I'm sure you're a nice guy, but let's just leave it at that."

The man looked puzzled. "I wasn't trying to make a move on you, Ms. Blackwell. I'm a fan, that's all. Sorry to have bothered you." He turned and walked back to his table. Enid left a five-dollar bill on the table and gathered her belongings.

When she walked outside, Deputy Barnes, who was assigned to watch her, was in his car in Sarah's parking lot. She walked over to him. "There's a creepy man at the back table. I think he's way too interested in me."

"I'll call it in if you think it's important."

"I wouldn't have mentioned it if I didn't." She sighed. "I'm sorry. I've been snapping at everyone today. I don't know if it's important, but it may be. I'm going back to the office." She pointed in the direction of the newspaper office. "I'm just going right there. I'll be fine."

As she started walking back to her office, she glanced over her shoulder. Deputy Barnes was driving slowly down the street behind her. And the man from Sarah's was also walking down the street. Enid picked up her pace and nearly jogged back.

When Deputy Barnes pulled into the parking lot, she pointed to where the man had been. "Did you see him? He was following me."

The deputy looked where Enid pointed. "No, sorry I don't see him."

Frustrated, Enid threw up her hands. "I'm going inside."

As she walked into her office, one of the cell phones in her tote vibrated. She had her old phone and the new burner phone Jack had given her. She pulled them both out, but it was her original phone ringing. She looked at the number and image on her screen and smiled. "Hello, Josh."

"You busy?"

"Never too busy for you. Is everything alright?"

"Well, that depends. If you can pick me up at the Columbia airport, then I won't have to spend the night here."

Enid wasn't sure she had heard him correctly. "Wait. You're here? In South Carolina?"

"Sure am. Sorry for the surprise. Well?"

Enid glanced at the time on her phone. "I can be there in about an hour."

"Great. I'll be at passenger pickup for American Airlines."

After the call, Enid looked for Jack but couldn't find him, so she jogged up to Ginger's desk. "I've got to leave, please let Jack know."

"You look excited. Anything I should know about?" Ginger asked.

Enid smiled. "Later." She told Deputy Barnes where she was going and told him he didn't have to follow her. He said he couldn't leave the county but would arrange for someone in Richland County to escort her.

"Don't be silly. I'm fine."

Traffic was heavier than usual, so it took her a little more than an hour to get to the airport. Heart pounding, she entered the passenger pickup lane and looked for Josh. When she saw him, he smiled and waved.

Within a few minutes, Josh was sitting next to her in the car. "I can't believe you're here," Enid said.

"You're even more beautiful than I remembered." He laid his head back against the seat and closed his eyes, so Enid drove in silence most of the way.

When they approached Madden, she murmured in a low voice, "You asleep?"

Josh opened his eyes. "No, just resting. It was a long flight and several long waits for connections. It's not easy to get here from New Mexico." He looked around. "Are we there?"

"Almost. I know you rented your place out, so do you want to go to my house?"

"I don't want to impose on you, and I didn't assume you'd take me in. I can stay at the inn."

"Don't be silly. If you don't have anywhere else to go, then we'll go to my place."

He squeezed her leg. "I accept your invitation."

CHAPTER 22

Josh insisted on putting his things in Enid's guest room, which also served as her home office. "I really don't want to barge in and assume anything."

Enid held him close to her. "I'm just so happy you're back." She pulled back. "Are you just visiting?"

"I honestly don't know. I have no job and no prospects. Tomorrow I'll look for a place to stay."

"You're more than welcome to stay here, but if you're just looking for a room, Mrs. Putnam mentioned she has one available."

"Who is she?"

"One of our reporters, the one who is missing, rented a garage apartment from Mrs. Putnam. But she has a big house and rents out a few rooms also."

Josh took her hand and led her to the bedroom. "You'll have to fill me in on everything, but let's do it tomorrow."

A knock on Enid's front door interrupted the moment. "I forgot to call Deputy Barnes and tell him I'm home. That's probably him. Wait here a minute." She peeped out and opened the door. "I'm so sorry. I forgot to call you."

"I saw you drive up. Just wanted to make sure you're alright. Was that, eh . . ."

"Yes, that was Josh Hart with me. So I'm safe for tonight. Why don't you go home?"

"Can't do that ma'am, but have a good evening," he said,

blushing slightly.

"Was that Pete's cousin?" Josh asked.

"Yes, he's watching the house—and me."

"Lucky guy."

"Ha. Very funny." She took his hand. "I think we were headed this way," she said as she directed him to the bedroom.

• • •

The next morning, Enid woke to the smell of bacon and coffee. She pulled on her jeans and walked into the kitchen. "You're up early."

"I was hungry. You didn't offer to feed me last night. How do you live here with no real food? I did find some bacon and eggs, though."

"That's been in the fridge for a few weeks, from the last time I had a guest." She didn't want to mention that she had cooked breakfast for Jack one morning. "Besides, I've got bagels, crackers, hummus, almonds, Pellegrino, tea."

"Like I said, no real food." He pointed to the table. "Have a seat and I'll get you some breakfast. And I don't want to hear any protests about animal rights. Two little strips of bacon won't kill you or destroy the planet."

Enid sat at the small dining table. "Yes, sir." She munched on a piece of bacon.

"If you'll wait, I'll give you some scrambled eggs to go with that." He pointed to the electric tea kettle. "There's hot water for you."

"I think you should stay here forever." She blushed. "Sorry, it was just a silly comment."

Josh leaned over and kissed the top of her head. "You're

allowed. And I didn't take it as a marriage proposal." He smiled. "Or was it?"

"Stop it. I'm hungry and you promised me eggs."

After eating, Josh gathered the dishes and put them in the sink. "I'll get these later. You've got a job. I don't. Well, maybe I do, actually. Do you have a minute? I want to run something past you."

"Of course."

"I had a conversation with John Stanholt."

"You mean the Bowman County sheriff, the one who took your job when you went to work for the governor's gang task force over a year ago?"

"Yes, the one and only Sheriff Stanholt. But I don't blame him for taking advantage of my bad decision. He got the job fair and square. Anyway, I approached him about hiring me as a deputy."

"What? Why would you do that?"

Josh laughed. "It's only temporary, and that's why he agreed to it."

"Wait. I'm totally confused. What's going on?"

"Before I explain, I want to repeat what I said yesterday. I'm not assuming anything about our relationship, and I'm not trying to rush things. But this guy who's after you isn't playing games, and I'm worried. The sheriff's department is down a couple of guys and tying up someone to cover you is a strain on their resources."

"I tried to tell them I didn't need anyone."

Josh held up his hand. "Let me finish. They're not just watching you to protect you, as important as that is. They also think this creep may show himself, and they'll nab him. But they also know he could go into hiding indefinitely. And Sheriff Stanholt simply doesn't have the manpower to provide protection for that long."

"So you're going to be my personal bodyguard. Is that it?"

Josh put his hand on hers. "I knew you wouldn't like the idea of me swooping in to protect you, but let's be practical. This solution is a way for me to figure out what I want to do, earn a little money, help the sheriff's office, and most importantly, protect the woman I love with all my heart. What's wrong with that?"

Enid leaned over and kissed him. "I don't deserve you." She looked at the time. "I've got to call Jack or get to the office soon. By the way, when does this arrangement of yours start?"

"Whenever you agree to it."

"Did you sell your pickup when you left for New Mexico?"

"Nah, I just loaned it to a buddy. He knows I'm back and plan to pick it up. I was kinda hoping you'd give me a ride over there."

Enid stood. "Then we need to get going. I'll call the office and let them know where I am."

CHAPTER 23

Just as Enid finished the last article for the paper's next edition, Jack walked into her office. "Well, I see you've already fired Deputy Barnes."

"Please tell me you didn't know about Josh's arrangement before I did."

"No, I just went out and had a chat with Josh in the parking lot this morning. I didn't know he was back in Madden."

"It surprised me too, to be honest. But I'm happy he's back."

"Josh told me about the deputy gig. Sounds like the perfect solution for everyone. For now, at least." Enid's office phone rang, and she glanced up at Jack.

"Go ahead and get it, we'll talk later," he said.

When she heard the caller's mechanically altered voice, a familiar dread crept through her body. "What do you want?"

"I know they're monitoring your calls, but by the time they get here, I'll be long gone. Where's your police protection?"

"I don't know what you're talking about."

"Enid, Enid, Enid," the voice said slowly. "Don't play games. We're too close to each other for that. It's just as well that he's gone. I wouldn't hurt you. How could I? You're my soulmate."

Enid shivered involuntarily. "If that's true, then why are you doing things that make me sad, like taking Winnie

Tucker and Mia Olson?"

"I told you. Were you not listening to me?" A slight pause. "I've got to go now." The line went dead. The phone rang again, but this time it was the SLED agent.

"He was calling from a cell phone, but we triangulated it and got the general location. Our guys are on the way now. We'll get him." Enid held her hands together to keep them from shaking.

She managed to focus on work again, until twenty minutes later when the phone rang. She held her breath and answered. "Please tell me it's over."

"I wish I could," the SLED agent said. "He left the phone for us to find. It's a burner, of course, and we're trying to find out now where it was sold and who purchased it." A pause. "And we found Mia Olson."

"Is she . . .?"

"I'm sorry. She's been dead a while. Probably killed her right after he abducted her. We'll contact her family. And we will get this guy. I promise."

Enid gasped. "Oh, no. Poor Mia. What about Winifred Tucker? Do you think . . .?" Enid couldn't bring herself to finish the sentence.

"I don't know, but I'll be honest, it doesn't look good. Not after this long."

After ending the call, Enid packed her tote to leave so she could work from home the rest of the day. Before leaving, she called Josh on his cell and told him what happened. "For now at least, this person thinks I no longer have a protective detail, so let's keep it that way. You head toward my house and wait down the road. I'll be leaving in a few minutes and then you can follow me."

Enid walked down to Jack's office and gave him the

news. He had tears in his eyes when she left him sitting at his desk. She hated to leave him alone, but she needed time to think. "Are you sure you'll be okay?"

Jack wiped his eyes. "Mia was so young and so full of energy. She wanted to work for the *Chicago Tribune*, and I promised her that when she was ready, I'd help her get an interview." He wiped his eyes again. "All we can do now is pray that Winnie will somehow be found alive."

CHAPTER 24

A short distance out of Madden on the road to Enid's house, Josh's pickup was pulled off on the side of the road in a small clearing, waiting for her. Enid kept driving and he pulled out to follow her at a safe distance in case anyone was watching.

Enid called her neighbor, just on the other side of the of the wooded area that separated the two houses, and he agreed to let Josh park his pickup on the property. To get to Enid's backyard, Josh just had to walk a short path through the woods. Thankfully, the neighbor didn't ask for an explanation, and she didn't offer one. He probably thought Josh was hiding his truck from either the repo man or a jealous wife.

Enid stayed in her car until she saw Josh emerging from the woods and walking toward her backyard. She went inside and unlocked the back door to let him in. Inside, he grabbed her and held her tight. "I don't like this set-up at all. Too many places for that nut whack to hide."

"You're assuming it's a guy. Isn't it possible a woman is the stalker?"

"One thing you learn in law enforcement is that anything is possible, but it's unusual for a woman to commit abduction of two females and to kill at least one of them. But you're right that until we know something more, we need to keep an open mind."

"I've got some things I want to share with you. Can we sit down and talk a few minutes?"

"You bet." Josh pulled her onto the sofa with him. "What's on your mind?"

"I got a call from Ty, the reporter."

"The one that's supposedly missing?"

"Yes, that one. He wanted me to meet him in Columbia."

"When was this?"

"Yesterday. With everything going on, I forgot to tell the SLED agent."

"His name is Whit Carlson. I've known him for years." He tapped her nose with his finger. "But I seriously doubt you forgot." He paused. "Wait, you're not . . . No, please don't do your own investigation. Not this time. You know this person tormenting you is crazy. Anything could happen."

"No, really. I just forgot. I was so irritated with Ty that I pushed him out of my mind."

"Where did he want you to meet him?"

"Well, here's the thing. He didn't give me a name or address of the place. He gave me GPS coordinates."

"Did you look them up?"

"Not yet. Let me get the note." She walked to the kitchen and retrieved it from the side pocket of her tote. "Here it is." She handed it to Josh.

He opened an app on his phone and input the information. "That's odd." He showed her his screen. "Do you know the area?"

Enid shook her head. "No, I've never been there.

"That looks like where the old rock quarry is located."

"Why would he want to meet me there?"

"I have no idea, but we need to tell Whit. I don't want to

get on his bad side by withholding information. Have you heard from Ty again?"

"No, I haven't."

"Is Ty on the up-and-up?"

"Ginger did a little snooping on him. He seems to be legit, but I'm beginning to wonder. He's certainly ambitious, I know that."

Josh grinned. "Gee, an ambitious reporter. Wonder who that describes?"

Enid hit his arm with her fist and made a face. "Stop it. I'm not ambitious and you know it. If I were, would I still be in Madden at a weekly paper?"

Josh leaned away from her slightly. "Why are you still here? At one time, I thought it was Jack holding you in Madden, but I think it's more than that."

Enid leaned her head back on the sofa. "You know how sometimes you want something so bad and then you have a chance to get it, but it's not as desirable as you had once thought?"

"What are you saying?"

"I'm saying if I had wanted to go back to work for a bigger, daily newspaper, I probably would have done so by now. When I came here to work for Jack, I thought it was a steppingstone to something bigger, to getting back to my old life. And then I realized staying in journalism wasn't what I really wanted."

"What do you want?"

"I don't know exactly."

"So you're stalling here until you figure it out."

"That's probably true, as much as I hate to admit it. You know Jack is probably going to sell the paper. The potential buyer, Darren Smoak, has already talked to me about staying."

"Well, I guess so. You're valuable to the paper. But why has Jack suddenly decided to sell? I thought news was in his blood."

"Jack said Darren approached him first, but I think the cancer scare made Jack realize there is more to life than work. He wants to travel and do other things than worry about deadlines. Maybe Darren is buying the paper for the same reason Jack did years ago. It's a way to stay in the news world without having to deal with the corporate crap that goes with it."

"How do you feel about all of this?"

"I'm still processing it. Amazingly, I'm not really upset. I understand Jack's situation. I just hope he finds someone. I hate to see him alone."

"What about his adopted daughter, Rachel?"

"She's away studying cybersecurity and will graduate soon. But I don't know if she'll come back to Madden. She'll have her own life to live."

Josh pulled her closer to him. "Well, Ms. Blackwell, I think you need to figure out what you want and live your own life too."

"And what about you? What do you want? For your life, I mean?"

"I'm trying to figure it out too. One thing I did figure out while I was in New Mexico is that I don't want to work for anyone in politics ever again. What an experience that was. In fact, I may not go back into law enforcement at all."

Enid shifted in her seat so she could face Josh. "So we may have solved our conflict-of-interest problem perma-nently. If I'm not a reporter and you're not in law enforcement, we don't have a problem."

Josh kissed her. "By George, you may be on to something."

CHAPTER 25

The news of Mia's death spread quickly and by the next morning, Madden was buzzing with news reporters from across South Carolina and elsewhere, including a news van from CNN. Jack suggested that Enid work from home to avoid the frenzy and the numerous requests for interviews. He also knew Josh would be close by.

Jack asked Ginger to take messages so he could return calls later. Part of him felt guilty for trying to avoid reporters. After all, news was his business, and he understood their push to get information. But the discovery of Mia's body had drained his energy.

A knock on his office door snapped him back to attention. He looked up and saw Darren Smoak grinning at him. "Hey, come on in."

Darren immediately planted himself in the chair across from Jack's desk. "It's crazy out there. Reminds me of the old days. Don't you miss the energy of reporting on breaking news?"

Jack managed a slightly crooked smile. "Not really." Jack studied Darren, who was clearly enjoying the carnival-like atmosphere in Madden. "I know we talked a bit about why you wanted to buy the paper, but mind if I ask you a few more questions?"

Darren frowned. "Not changing your mind are you? Or is a murder in town driving your price up?"

Jack chuckled. "You've offered a generous price. In fact, you may be overpaying me. My attorney is looking at the contract now. Far as I know, we're still good to go."

Darren waved his hand at Jack and shrugged. "My offer is worth it. You've done a good job building up readership in the tri-county area. And that reporter of yours, Enid Blackwell. She's the topping on the cake."

Jack bristled, trying to remember if Darren had always been sexist. "Has she indicated to you that she'll stay?"

"Not yet, but she will. I'll make the job so attractive she won't even think about leaving."

Jack smiled to himself. "Well, if that's what she wants, I hope you work out a good deal for her. If I have any regrets, it's that I feel like I've let her down."

"Why is that?" Darren paused and then grinned. "Wait, you two aren't, you know, an item?"

"Not that it would be any of your business, but no. We're just close friends. Besides, she's in a relationship."

"Oh? She didn't mention it when we talked."

Why did Darren think she would? Jack decided to drop the subject. "Anyway, what I wanted to know is why, after all these years, you decided to buy a paper. As I recall, you couldn't wait to get out of the news business."

"Well, I was young and foolish. Now I'm somewhat older and a lot more foolish." Darrel laughed heartily at his own joke. "People change. Do you want the same things now you wanted twenty years ago?"

"Actually, I do, pretty much. But I'm a lot simpler guy than you."

Darren leaned forward slightly and lowered his voice. "By the way, I was sorry to hear about your wife's death. Cancer, was it?"

"Thank you. Yes, it was." Jack pushed the memories back before they overcame him. "Enid tells me you plan to go full digital."

"Nobody does print these days. It costs too much. Only old people want to hold a paper in their hands."

"I'm sure she explained that you'll lose those 'old people' readers, which is the bulk of our subscription base. Are you prepared financially to deal with that?"

Darren's eyes narrowed. "I'm touched that you're concerned about my finances, but you needn't be. Besides, Madden is growing like crazy with that new distribution center just down the road. Who knows, maybe we'll even become a daily paper." Darren stood up. "Look, unless you've got more questions, I need to get out of your way. I'd like to introduce myself to the reporters in town as the new owner of the *Tri-County Gazette*, if that's okay with you. You know, get connected with them."

"I'd rather you not do that. It's premature. Besides, I need to inform our readers first. And I need to sign the contract, of course, to make it official."

Darren shrugged. "Whatever. Take it easy, Jack. See 'ya later." Darren smiled like a politician, but something in Darren's eyes made Jack uneasy.

"I'll get back to you as soon as I hear from my attorney," Jack said. Darren threw up his hand in acknowledgement as he walked out of Jack's office.

CHAPTER 26

Enid was working at the small desk in her combination office and guest room. She silenced her email notifications and phone calls so she could get some work done. Josh was outside trimming the bushes near her house to eliminate possible hiding spots for anyone lurking.

Feeling the urge for a cup of tea, Enid got up and went to the kitchen. When she returned to her desk, she checked her messages and emails. One in particular caught her attention. The sender was someone named Talon. Just the single name. But it was the subject line that caught her attention: "You Are the News."

She opened the email and read it: "Here's a collection of your work I compiled for you. You should be proud!"

A PDF file was attached to the email. Enid ran a virus check and then opened it. The file was a selection of nearly two hundred pages of her previous work, beginning with her most recent articles from the previous year about the search for Madden's town historian, Catherine Murray. She scrolled down to the last pages and found a series of articles written for her college newspaper nearly fifteen years ago. How would anyone know about those articles? Her name wasn't Blackwell then, although she and Cade Blackwell shared the byline on a few of the articles. Working with him spawned a relationship that eventually ended up in marriage—and then a divorce ten years later. The sender also included an article she had written for an internal newsletter at a bank in Charlotte where she worked after leaving the Associated Press.

Her reading was interrupted by the sound of the back door opening. "Josh, is that you?"

"Yes, it's me. I'm going to take a shower. Worked up a sweat trimming those bushes around your bedroom windows."

"Can you come here a minute first? I've got something to show you."

When Josh walked into the room, she pointed to the PDF file on her screen. "I just got this."

"What is it?"

"A bunch of my old articles."

"Who sent it?"

"Someone named Talon."

"You mean like a bird's claw?"

Enid nodded. "Look at this collection. Some of these go back to my college and banking days."

"That's weird. Do you know anyone by that name?"

"No, I would have remembered a name like Talon. While you take a shower, I'm going to send this to Cade to look at. Maybe he'll remember this person."

"I think you need to send it to Whit at SLED. I mean, look at that subject line. Isn't that exactly what the stalker said to you?"

"I'll send it to both of them."

Josh kneeled beside Enid's chair so that his face was inches from hers. "I don't like that look on your face. I know you want to investigate all of this yourself, but this is dangerous. Your co-worker is dead, and there's still a missing girl out there. You've got to promise me you won't interfere or try anything on your own."

"I love that you worry about me, and I promise to be careful."

"I guess that's the best I'll get from you." Josh stood and headed to the bathroom.

Enid waited for Josh to close the bathroom door and then tapped on Cade's cell phone number in her favorites list. With five hours difference in time, it would be mid-afternoon in London. After several rings, a female voice with a British accent answered. "Hello."

Caught off guard, Enid stammered. "I'm sorry . . . I'm . . . I'm trying to reach Cade Blackwell. Did I get the wrong number?"

"Oh, no, luv. He's here. May I say who is ringing?"

"It's . . . I'm Enid. His ex-wife."

"Oh, alright then, hold a bit."

Even though Enid was happy for Cade, somewhere inside, she was also envious of the woman he was going to marry. It wasn't that Enid wanted to be married to Cade. What she did want was a permanent home, someone to share her life with. The way she and Cade used to.

"Enid? Is that you?" With her speaker on, Cade's voice filled the room, just like he was sitting across from her.

She turned off the speaker. "Hello, Cade. I'm sorry to interrupt you at home. I didn't expect to get your fiancé."

Cade's familiar laughter shot through the airwaves. "That was my research assistant, Olivia. I left my phone on my desk and told her to answer as I was expecting a call. But certainly not from you."

Enid wasn't sure why, but she was relieved the woman wasn't who he was going to marry. "If you're busy we can talk later."

"No, don't be silly. I'm never too busy for you. Is every-thing alright there or did you just realize you can't live without me?" A slight pause. "Sorry, that was a bad joke. But seriously, are you okay?"

"Well, yes and no. I'm being stalked."

"Stalked? Are you sure? Never mind, of course you're sure. Let me shut my office door, and then you can tell me what's going on."

Enid told Cade about Winifred's and Mia's disappear-ances, and about the discovery of Mia's body.

"I'm so sorry. But why is this guy stalking you now? Do you have protection?"

"Yes, I have a deputy assigned to me." Enid failed to mention it was Josh Hart, whom Cade had met several times before he left for London. "I want to send you a PDF to your personal email. It's safe. I ran a virus check on it." She hit the send button. "Let me know when you get it."

"Hold on, let me check on my phone. I can't use my per-sonal account at work."

In less than a minute, Enid heard a pinging noise. "Ah, here it is," Cade said. "That didn't take long. It's a big file. What's in it?"

"Apparently my stalker had been collecting copies of my work. When he first contacted me, he said he wanted to make me the news. That's the subject line of his email. It was sent by someone named Talon. Do you know anyone by that name? Might be a nickname."

"Not that I recall. These articles go back to our college newspaper days. Do you think it's someone we went to school with?"

"I have no idea. I was hoping you might."

"And this guy is the same person who kidnapped those

two people?" Cade asked.

"We don't know, but probably."

"You need to give this to whomever is investigating the case. They may be able to trace the source of the email, but I doubt the sender would be that careless. Did you save any of your yearbooks? I Marie Kondo'd all my stuff when I left the country."

"I did the same thing, after you and I . . ." Enid cleared her throat. "I don't think I have any of that stuff left, but maybe I can find it online or ask the school to help."

Cade laughed. "Wait, you don't need to do any of that. Let the investigators earn their salaries."

"Stop lecturing me, please. If you think of anything, let me know. Okay?"

"I will. And please be careful. I still care about you."

Enid wasn't sure how to respond. "I'll let you know if anything changes. 'Bye, Cade." She hung up before he could reply.

• • •

Enid called Agent Carlson and then sent him the PDF, promising to let him know if she found out anything else. While she had been talking to Carlson, someone left a phone message:

"Ms. Blackwell, this is Winifred Tucker's mother. When you get this, please give me a call on this number only. The police are monitoring my home phone, but they know I use this cell for friends and family. Please, it's urgent."

Enid tapped on the telephone icon to return the call. "Mrs. Tucker, this is Enid. What's happened?" She couldn't bring herself to ask if they found Winifred.

"The person who took Winnie wants to talk to you. He says you pushed him away, so he won't release Winnie."

"How did he get in touch with you? Aren't they monitoring your calls?"

"Yes, but not this line. I have no idea how he got my private cell number." she hesitated. "I wanted to ask you to help me. Maybe he's lying, but if there's any chance he'll let Winnie go, then . . ." Her voice trailed off and Enid heard a stifled sob.

"Mrs. Tucker, I'll do anything I can to help you find Winnie. But you can't believe this person. We have to assume he's lying. I don't want you to build up your hope."

"You think she's dead, don't you?"

Enid hesitated. "I don't know, but tell me how I'm supposed to talk to him. My calls are monitored."

"He says his name is Talon and that you would recognize that name. Do you know him?"

"No, but he sent me an email. What else did he say?"

"He's sending you a message on something . . . wait, let me look at my note. Here it is, it's called SecureDrop. Of course, he said not to tell the police anything about this." Another pause. "Will you please contact him for me? Please? I know it's asking a lot, and the authorities will be furious with both of us, but I'm sure you understand that I'll do whatever it takes to get my child back."

Enid's pulse was racing. How did she become the object of this stalker's attention? And why did he have to kill Mia and . . . She couldn't finish the thought. There was no reason to assume Winifred Tucker was alive, and every reason to believe Talon was playing a game with them.

"I'll do what I can. Can I call you back on this number?" Enid also gave Mrs. Tucker her burner number that only a few people had. "Don't give that number to anyone else."

CHAPTER 27

After talking to Mrs. Tucker, Enid immediately called Jack. "How can I get access to SecureDrop?"

"You mean the program that's used for confidential informants?"

"I've never used it, but I know Cade does. Can I install it?"

"Stay there," Jack said. "I'm coming over. We need to talk."

When Jack arrived about twenty minutes later, Enid and Josh were sitting at her small dining table. "What's going on?" Jack asked.

"Have a cup of coffee and join us," Enid said. "Don't worry, Josh made it, so it should be good."

Josh turned to Enid. "Would you like for me to leave so you two can talk?"

"I have no secrets from you, and you need to know what's happening too."

Josh pulled his chair away from the table as far as he could. "I'll just sit back and listen, then."

Jack got a cup of coffee from the coffeemaker on the counter and sat down with Enid. "Why do you need to use SecureDrop?"

Enid glanced at Josh. "I need to tell you what's happened. Please don't overreact."

Josh shrugged. "I'll try."

"Jack, Talon has contacted Mrs. Tucker and told her he won't let Mia go until I make contact with him through Se-cureDrop."

"Why would you believe Winifred is still alive? He killed Mia, and I'd bet Winifred is dead too."

Enid took a sip of tea. "I know. But I can't ignore Mrs. Tucker's plea. I just can't. Don't you understand that?"

Josh raised his hand. "May I speak?" Without waiting for a reply, he continued. "I don't like where this is going. You're working behind SLED's back. That could get you killed." Josh looked at Jack. "You could become complicit in this crime as well. As would I."

Enid slammed her hands on the table. "Stop it, both of you. I'm not going to meet this guy on some dark road at night. He's asked me to communicate with him through a secure message service."

"And you can do that with law enforcement's support," Josh said.

Jack raised his hand. "Okay, guys, let's calm down and walk through this. Enid, you asked me about SecureDrop. We can get access to install it through the Freedom of the Press Foundation." He turned to Josh. "Just so you'll know, it's set up on the dark web using the Tor browser. Journal-ists, whistleblowers, and informants use it to exchange confidential information." He looked at Enid. "Getting ac-cess is not the problem. But I agree with Josh. The problem is your getting involved without Agent Carlson's knowledge, which could put us all in their crosshairs. And Darren Smoak needs to know also, as the paper could get pulled into this. We could all be in big trouble."

"And Winnie could be alive, and Talon could be telling the truth," Enid said. "I couldn't live with myself if I didn't at least try to help bring Winnie home." She paused. "But here's a question I have. How would Talon know about SecureDrop? Does that mean he's a journalist himself? I mean, the average person on the street has probably never heard of it."

"That's a good question," Jack said. "It would also explain his obsession with you. Maybe it's a professional obsession."

"Or maybe Ty is orchestrating this set-up," she said.

"You mean Ty could be Talon?" Jack asked.

"I don't know, but we know Ty has been in contact with Talon. Ty's been trying to manipulate this situation from the beginning and has an inside source. He's after an exclusive, and he needs me to keep Talon close to him." She looked at Jack and then Josh. "Or he is Talon."

Josh stood up. "Let me at least have an off-the-record conversation with Whit Carlson at SLED. We go way back. I can't promise what his reaction will be, but I might be able to buy us a little time."

"I'm okay with that but only after I make first contact. I promised Mrs. Tucker," Enid said. "Then you can talk with Whit."

Jack stood and put his coffee cup in the sink. "That was good coffee. And I'll talk with Darren."

"No need to do that," Enid said. "I'll talk to him, but I'm not going to tell him about all this. There's no need to put the paper at risk or ask him to support what I'm doing. I'm going to tell him I quit."

CHAPTER 28

After Jack left, Josh put his arms around Enid. "I'm sorry if I preached to you. I just worry that you're going to get in over your head and something bad will happen. I don't want to lose you."

Enid kissed him and pulled away. "I know you worry, and I'm sorry to upset you."

"Are you really going to quit the *Tri-County Gazette?* You're not someone who reacts spontaneously, so you must have already made that decision before talking with Jack."

"You know me pretty well. If I'm honest with myself, I made the decision after my conversation with Darren."

"Sounds like you two didn't hit it off too good."

"He's right about the paper. To survive, it needs to go digital. But it'll be a different paper altogether."

Josh pushed a strand of hair away from her face. "You enjoy a challenge. Are you sure you don't want to stay and help him build his vision?"

"I'm not leaving because of Darren. I'm leaving because of me. I need to find out who I really am."

"Will you move from Madden?"

Enid smiled. "I like it here, but I haven't thought it through completely." She gathered their cups and saucers and put them in the sink with Jack's. "I'll get these later. I need to call Darren and set up a meeting."

• • •

When Josh and Enid arrived at the newspaper office a few hours later, Josh pulled into a parking space next to the building. "It's not too late to change your mind," Josh said.

"I know, but it's really what I want to do."

"Then go do it. I'll wait here in the car."

When Enid walked into the office, Ginger met her at the door. "What the hell is going on?"

"What do you mean?"

"You're working from home, and Jack just called and said he wasn't going to be back today. Reporters are trying to reach you and Jack. Nobody tells me anything!"

Enid would miss Ginger. Despite her outbursts and occasional strange behavior, she was a good worker with great research skills. "I'm sorry. We'll talk later. Right now, I've got a meeting with Darren Smoak. We're supposed to meet in my office."

"Darren The Wonderful, you mean? There's something about that guy I don't like. Please tell me he's not going to be my new boss."

Enid smiled. "Okay, I won't tell you. But seriously, I'll catch up with you soon. We'll get together at Sarah's."

Ginger pretended to pout. "Alright, if you promise." She pointed down the hallway. "His Majesty, Mr. Smoak, awaits in your office."

Enid took a deep breath and walked down the hall. Her office door was closed, which upset her. It was her office, and she would decide if the door should be shut. *Don't look for a fight. Just resign.* She stopped herself from knocking on her office door and instead just walked in. Darren was sitting at her desk, as if she had already left. "Hello. Am I late?"

Darren stood. "No, I was just making some phone calls. Hope you don't mind."

Enid stood silently until Darren got up. "Thank you for meeting with me on such short notice," she said.

Taking a seat in the chair across from Enid's desk, Darren flashed his best smile. "No problem at all. I hope you're ready to work with me on building this paper to its full potential."

"Actually, I do want to talk about the job. I think your vision has merit, and I hope it works out for you and for Madden. This paper has been an institution for keeping the citizens informed of local news."

"Great, I'm glad we're in agreement."

"But I turned in my resignation to Jack earlier today. I'm leaving the paper."

"But . . ." Darren's face reflected his shock. "I thought . . ."

"I will work as a contractor to help Jack through the transition, if he wants me to, but once the sale is final, I'll leave."

"But why?"

"I have my reasons, which have nothing to do with you or your vision. Whether I like all-digital formats or not, it is the future. I'm aware of that. My reasons for leaving are personal."

Darren sat up in his chair and focused on renewing the crease in his pressed khaki pants. "Naturally, I'm disappointed. In fact, Ty and I were talking about you just yesterday."

"Ty? You mean the *State* reporter? I didn't know you knew him."

"We've just recently met. He told me he had proposed

an exclusive agreement, but you haven't agreed to it. Not yet."

"Nor do I intend to." Enid paused to compose her thoughts. "I really don't like the idea of your discussing my work outside of this office. You don't own this paper yet, and you have no reason to get involved." Enid straightened a stack of papers on her desk. "Anyway, I just wanted to give you the courtesy of letting you know I won't be staying. Again, I appreciate your coming in to meet with me on short notice. I'm sorry I couldn't give you the answer you wanted." Enid stood and held out her hand. "Good luck, Darren. I hope your vision gives you what you want."

Darren stood and gave Enid a weak handshake. "Good luck to you as well." He walked toward the door but then turned back to her. "Are you going to work at another paper?"

"I'm not ready to disclose my plans at this time. Goodbye, Darren."

As soon as Darren left, Enid sat down to type a formal resignation. She wanted to give Jack the assurance that whatever came of this business with Talon, the paper would not be involved, or at least not held accountable for her actions. She wiped the tears that spilled onto her cheeks and began to create the document that would end her employment with the *Tri-County Gazette*. She would also sign a Hold Harmless Agreement to protect the paper from liability from anything she did as a contractor working for the paper. But as she typed, her mind kept drifting back to Ty and Darren. How and why did they meet?

CHAPTER 29

The next morning, Enid walked into Jack's office and handed him a large envelope. "Here's my resignation and a Hold Harmless Agreement. I'd like to stay on as a contractor until the sale goes through, but since I won't be an employee, the paper can distance itself from my actions, if needed."

Jack laid the envelope on his desk. "Are you sure about all this?"

"It's time I figured out my life, don't you think?" I mean, while you're going fly fishing and checking off your bucket list, I have a few things on my list too."

"Promise me that you won't do anything dangerous. I'm worried about your making contact with this Talon fella. You need to work with SLED and the sheriff's office."

"I promise to be careful. But I have to do whatever I can to help Winnie. For whatever reason, Talon has involved me, and I can't ignore that. You understand, don't you?"

Jack smiled slightly. "I'm afraid I understand completely. That's why I can't argue with you, so I'll accept your resignation and hire you as an independent contractor for as long as I own the paper. I'll get Ginger to complete the contractor agreement so you can sign it."

"How's the contract coming along? Do you have a sale date for the paper yet?"

Jack shook his head. "My attorney has found a few

'irregularities,' as he called them, in Darren's financial records. He says it's probably nothing, but he wants to check a little deeper. By the way, do you still want access to SecureDrop? I'll get it set up on your laptop."

Enid reached into the large leather tote bag on the floor beside her chair and pulled out a small laptop. "I'd like to begin using my own laptop, since I'm a contractor now. You can install it on this one."

Jack took the laptop from her. "Ginger can do it now if you want to wait. Or I can drop it off later."

"I need to contact Talon right away."

"Okay, then. I'll bring it to your office as soon as she finishes. Do you need her to go over the instructions?"

"No, I think I can figure it out with their online journalist's guide, but I'll let her know if I get stuck. While I wait, I'll see if Josh would like to go with me to Sarah's."

"Must be nice to have a personal bodyguard."

Enid smiled. "Yes, it is."

• • •

When Enid and Josh got to Sarah's, it was nearly empty, with only a handful of people. One of them was the man who talked to Enid previously, and he was at her usual table again. She whispered to Josh. "That's my admirer. He keeps inviting me to join him. Hopefully, when he sees you, he'll get the message."

Josh took the lead and Enid followed him to a table on the opposite side of the seating area. She was careful to avoid eye contact with the man. But once she got her tea, she glanced at him over the top of the cup as she sipped. He was staring at her. "That guy gives me the creeps. But don't turn around. He's looking this way."

"All the more reason for me to look," Josh said as he turned in his seat. The man nodded to Josh in acknowledgment. "I'll be right back," Josh said.

As Josh approached the man's table, he stood and offered his hand to Josh. "Hello, I'd invite you to join me, but it seems you already have company," the man said. "Of course, you're both welcome to sit with me."

"My name is Josh Hart. And your name?"

The man cleared his throat and briefly shifted his gaze away from Josh. "It's Seth. I work for the distribution center." He cleared his throat again. "Actually, I do IT work for them as a contractor. You know, network maintenance, workstations, that kind of stuff. And what do you do? I haven't seen you around here, as I recall."

"You might say I'm a contractor also. I'm working on a special assignment. Our mutual friend Ms. Blackwell says you're in here often. Funny that you always choose the table she uses regularly. Not that she owns it or anything. It's just that with all these empty tables, what a coincidence," Josh said, waving his arm around the room.

Seth shifted his weight and crossed his arms on his chest. "I wasn't aware this was her table. I'll be sure to choose another one next time."

"No problem. As I said, she doesn't own it. I was just commenting on the coincidence. You have a nice day. See you next time."

"What was that all about?" Enid asked when Josh returned to their table.

"Just getting to know one of the regulars here."

CHAPTER 30

Later that afternoon, Enid turned on her personal laptop with the SecureDrop Journalist Workstation USB drive and Tor browser now installed. She then called Mrs. Tucker on her personal line. "I'm set up to communicate with the kidnapper now. If he calls you again, tell him to use his code name Talon. He seems to be familiar with the SecureDrop platform, so he'll know how to use it."

"I have no idea what you're talking about, but hopefully he will. Why does he call himself Talon?"

"I think it's just a code name." Enid didn't want to pull Mrs. Tucker into Talon's game any further than she had to.

"Thank you for doing this. I know it's asking a lot, and I don't like working behind law enforcement's back any more than you do. But if it'll bring Winnie home, we have to do this."

"I can't blame you. If I learn anything from him, I'll let you know."

After talking to Mrs. Tucker, Enid decided to call the University of South Carolina School of Journalism, where she and Cade met while completing the graduate program. The woman who answered seemed confused by Enid's question. "Is that T-a-l-o-n?"

"Yes," Enid said. "I don't know if that's a nickname or a first or last name. Can you please check enrollment for the years I gave you?"

"It'll take me a little while. Do you want me to call you back later?"

"No, I'll wait."

A loud sigh. "Okay, then hold please."

While Enid was waiting, she checked the SecureDrop account even though she had set it up to be notified if anything came through. Nothing.

"Are you still there?" the woman asked.

"Yes, I'm here. Did you find anything with that name?"

"Nobody with the name Talon in that timeframe."

"Well, thanks for checking."

Just as she ended the call, a notification came through that someone had left a message via SecureDrop. She read the message:

"I'm so happy to finally connect with you, Enid. You have no idea how honored I am to work with you. But first, I guess you want to know about young Miss Tucker. She's so sweet, but she does miss her mother. By the way, did you enjoy the collection of your articles I sent you? It took me a little while to find some of them, but it was a labor of love, as they say. I just want you to get the recognition you deserve. You work with me and I'll let Miss Tucker go home. Is that a deal? Oh, and by the way, don't share our secrets chats with those county and state police idiots. I wouldn't want anything to happen to our young friend because you screwed up. Your fan, Talon."

Enid's hands trembled as she read the message again. When Josh walked in, she jumped at the sound of his voice.

"Sorry, didn't mean to startle you." He walked toward her. "What's wrong? You look like you've seen a ghost."

She pointed to the computer screen. "Here, read this."

Josh sat in the chair beside Enid. "Whoa. This is serious.

Who is this nut job?" He pulled out his cell phone.

"Who are you calling?"

"Whit Carlson. He needs to know about this."

"No, wait. Didn't you read what Talon said?"

Josh lowered his phone. "You can't seriously be considering keeping this to yourself. He's a deranged killer, and you could be next." He took her hands in his. "Look, I know you're trying to do the right thing, but let me talk to Whit off the record. He'll know what to do."

"If something happens to Winnie because we talked to the police, I'll never be able to forgive myself."

• • •

Josh tapped on Whit Carlson's personal number in his contacts. "Hey, Whit, this is Josh Hart. Got a minute?"

"Sure. What's up."

"Are you where you can talk privately?"

"Hold on. I will be in a minute." Josh could hear footsteps as Whit moved to a more secure spot. "Okay, I'm alone now. What's going on?"

"Can we talk off the record?"

"Oh, man, I hate it when people ask that. You know nothing is off the record with us."

Josh was silent, knowing how Enid would react if he blew this conversation with Whit. "Then I can't talk to you. I gave my word it would be off the record."

Whit laughed. "Love has got you messed up, man. Really messed up. Have you forgotten you're a lawman too?"

"It's just temporary for now. My law enforcement days are likely over."

"Well shit, man. Okay. Then we're off the record, for

now. But if I don't feel comfortable with what you tell me, we'll forget it happened and I don't want to hear anything else unofficially. Got it?"

"Got it." Josh told Whit about Enid's contact with Talon and about the collection of articles he sent.

"Does she have any idea who he is?"

"No. She thought it might be someone she went to journalism school with, but she's done some research and hasn't been able to find anyone with that name."

"Well, of course he's not going to use his real name. I need for her to send me those messages right away."

"What will you do with them? Turn them over to the FBI? I heard you pulled them into the case."

"For now, they're just doing some profiling. But look, you're making me the bad guy here. I'm just trying to help. Besides, you came to me. What do you want me to do? Run a covert operation?"

Josh sighed. "You're right. I'm sorry. It's just that this whole mess is unbelievable. Why did he pick Enid?"

"She's in the public eye, and there seem to be more crazies out there than ever. It doesn't help that she's an attractive woman. I'll do what I can to keep this tamped down, but I can't withhold it from the FBI. That'd be my job, man. You're too close to Enid to make these decisions. That's understandable, but let's follow protocol."

"Let me talk to Enid. You'll get the messages later today."

CHAPTER 31

Enid crossed her arms on her chest. "No, I won't send my messages to Whit. I know how these things work. They'll blow it, and Winnie may get killed." She stared at Josh. "You promised it would be off the record."

Josh spent the next ten minutes explaining to Enid why they had to get SLED involved. "We can't do this alone. It's too big and too dangerous."

"I hope you're right. In fact, you'd better be right. I'll send Talon's messages to Whit, and then I want to check out that guy at Sarah's. What did you say his name is?"

"Seth, that's all he told me. He wasn't very forthcoming with information. Do you think he could be Talon?"

"I'm not making any assumptions at this point, but he gives me the creeps."

"While you snoop around on Seth, I'm going to do a perimeter check for footprints or any sign of activity around your yard and the woods." He kissed Enid's lips lightly. "Got to keep you safe."

After Josh left, Enid got the number for the distribution center and hit the extension for human resources on the automated phone system. When a woman answered, Enid asked to speak to someone about one of their contractors. After being on hold for several minutes, she then got cut off. Frustrated, she grabbed her tote and jacket and went to look for Josh. When he saw her, he began walking back to the house. "Nothing unusual around here. A few deer tracks. Looks like they've been chewing on your bushes again." He looked at her tote. "You going somewhere?"

"I'm going to the distribution center. Couldn't get anything by phone."

"I'll go with you. You drive and I'll stay low in the back seat."

• • •

The guard at the entrance to the distribution center gave Enid a visitor pass. "He with you?" the guard asked, looking in the back seat at Josh.

"Hi, buddy," Josh said smiling. "I'm just the bodyguard."

The gate guard frowned. "Don't forget to stop by here and turn in your pass on the way out."

"Of course," said Enid. When they drove away, she and Josh both laughed. "Like there's another way to get out of here without going through this gate," she said. "You going in with me?"

"No, I think I'll stay here and observe."

Enid was greeted at the entrance by a security guard, and she told him she needed to go to Human Resources. He gave her a visitor badge and directed her down the hallway, first door on the left. As Enid walked toward her destination, she could feel the guard watching her from behind.

"I'm here to talk to someone about one of your contractors," Enid told the woman at the front desk and was instructed to wait for someone to help her.

About ten minutes later, a young man came out of an office and walked toward her. "Ms. Blackwell, how can I help you?"

"I'd like some information on one of your contractors." Enid showed him her press credentials, hoping to encourage him to help her.

The young man, who introduced himself as Edward, not Ed, he cautioned, took Enid to his small, windowless office. "Please have a seat and tell me more about why you need this information."

Deciding that honesty was the best policy, Enid explained, "This man, his first name is Seth, has taken an unusual interest in my work. I'm not here to file any kind of complaint. For reasons I can't elaborate on right now, I just need to know if this guy is legitimate. Does he really work here?"

Edward seemed to be studying Enid intently, as if trying to decide if she herself was legitimate. "Well, I guess I can tell you that, at least." He leaned in and lowered his voice. "Just don't tell anyone." He slapped his palms to his face. "And for God's sake, don't print this information."

Enid laughed. "Don't worry. Your secret is safe. Seth said he works in Information Technology. I imagine you get a lot of contractors working in that area."

Edward was intently studying his computer screen. "I'm sorry, I don't have anyone with the first or middle name Seth working as a contractor. Are you sure that's correct?"

"No, but that's all he offered."

"Let me check the regular employees." Edward punched away at this keyboard. His forehead scrunched in concentration. "We had an employee here recently whose name was Seth, and he worked in our IT department as a programmer." He shifted his gaze from the keyboard to Enid. "But he left about six months ago."

"Did he leave voluntarily?"

Edward grinned. "Now, you know I can't tell you that." He leaned in again and whispered. "Let's just say, we probably wouldn't hire him again." He stood up from his desk and said in a more formal tone. "If that's all you needed then?" He stared at Enid until she rose.

"Thanks, Edward. You've been a big help." Enid added in a whisper. "And this is our secret."

After turning in her visitor badge, Enid returned to the car. Josh was slumped down in the back seat looking around the parking lot. "Well, did you find him?" he asked.

Enid threw her tote on the front seat and got in, fastening her seat belt before she replied. "Maybe."

"Maybe? What does that mean exactly?"

"It means they had no record of Seth as a contractor, but they had an employee named Seth who left about six months ago. And I got the impression he may have been fired or at least forced to resign."

"I'm beginning to wonder if Seth gave us his actual name. Maybe he made it up."

"Or maybe he's a disgruntled employee out for revenge. In any event, I can't imagine what I could have done to him to make him target me."

CHAPTER 32

When Enid saw whose name appeared on her phone screen, she almost didn't answer. What could she say to Mrs. Tucker that wouldn't give her false hope? Or crush her spirit? "Hello, Mrs. Tucker."

"Don't you think it's about time you called me Julia?"

"Okay, Julia it is then. How are you?" Dumb question to ask the mother of a kidnapped child. "Sorry, I didn't mean to . . . just a habit. I can't imagine how you must be feeling."

"It's okay. I didn't take offense." She paused. "Have you contacted that monster who took Winnie?"

"I have, but I want to tell you something first. The SLED agent knows about the SecureDrop account. I've sent him the message I exchanged with the suspected kidnapper."

"You mean Talon. Isn't that what he calls himself?"

"Yes, at least we assume it's him. I promise you we'll do everything we can to protect Winnie. And I'll do everything I can to help you."

A long sigh. "I guess it was asking too much of you or anyone to keep that information to yourself. You know, this morning, I caught myself referring to Winnie in the past tense. When I realized what I had done, I burst into tears. I'm just having a hard time clinging to hope. Everyone says the first forty-eight hours are critical, and we've passed that point."

"There are plenty of exceptions, and we're all doing all

we can to get her back." Enid stopped short of making promises beyond her control. "At least we've opened up communications with him." She paused. "He says Winnie is fine and misses you. Of course, we don't know that message is actually from her."

Julia sobbed loudly and then blew her nose. "I'm sorry. Maybe it's not real, but it's still comforting. I miss her so much." She blew her nose again. "Oh, I wanted to tell you they found Chad, my stable manager."

"I've been wondering about him. Do they think he's involved?"

"I don't think so. He's from Kentucky and skipped town to avoid some debts. He panicked when all this happened and figured he'd get arrested. Agent Carlson said he was cleared as a suspect for Winnie's abduction."

"But did Chad see or know anything? After all, he was the last one to talk to Winnie and to Mia."

"I hate that nice reporter was killed. She was only trying to do her job, and then . . ."

Enid heard Julia crying softly.

"I'm sorry to be so emotional today. All of this is getting to me, I guess. All I know is Agent Carlson said he's reasonably sure Chad had nothing to do with any of this. But they are going to keep an eye on him, just in case. Chad came back here to apologize for leaving so abruptly. He knows I rely on him to keep the horses and stable in order. I'm going to advance him some money to pay off his debt so he can work here again. It's hard to find a good stable person these days, and I always liked him."

"Are you sure that's a good idea? I mean, until they totally clear him of any involvement."

"Chad knows he'll be under a microscope for a while, but

I think he's glad to be back. And I sure need him. I've been trying to manage the stables myself, just to stay busy. But it's more than I can, or want, to handle. Horses are Winnie's passion, not mine."

"I'd like to talk to Chad. Do you think that's possible?" Enid asked.

Julia didn't respond immediately. "Well, I guess it's alright. I mean, you're helping me, so it's the least I can do. Why don't you come here and meet with him at the stables? Might be more private that way."

"Don't mention it to Agent Carlson or anyone else. They don't appreciate reporters meddling."

CHAPTER 33

At Enid's insistence, Josh followed her at a distance and parked on the highway, out of sight. She needed to make Chad feel comfortable about talking with her. He was brushing down a beautiful gray and white Arabian horse when Enid arrived. The smell of fresh hay made the world seem right somehow. The stables brought back memories of when she was a young girl and insisted on taking riding lessons. Her mother found a place not too far away, and Enid rode every Saturday for nearly a year until her horse got stung by a bee and threw her onto the dirt path. She broke her arm in the fall and her mother made her give up riding.

"Thank you for meeting with me, Chad. I want to assure you I'm not here writing a story or anything like that. In fact, I've left the paper. I'm just helping Julia, Mrs. Tucker."

"Yes, ma'am. Mrs. Tucker told me the same thing. But I don't know anything. If I had, I would have told the SLED agent and that county investigator."

"You may remember something that got pushed to the back of your mind. It's like how sometimes we shove a box of things to the back of the closet and forget about it until later." She paused. "Can I ask you a few questions?"

Chad nodded.

"Tell me about the day Winnie was taken."

Chad leaned forward and put his face in his hands before he sat up again and spoke. "She's a good kid, always polite.

And she loves her horses. She always asks questions about how to take care of them. She has a way with them too. I used to call her the little horse whisperer." He cleared his throat. "She likes that."

Enid let Chad set the pace for their conversation. She was afraid pushing him might make him back off.

Chad sat up straight in the chair and continued. "That afternoon, nothing was unusual. Miss Winnie went for a ride, came back, and I told her I'd brush Hero down. That's her favorite horse," he said, motioning to the horse he had been grooming. "I knew Miss Winnie had homework to do, but she wanted to take care of him herself. It was nearly dark when she left to go back to the house. That's the last I saw her, walking down the road back to the house."

"Had you seen anything unusual that day? Or had anyone been hanging around the stable?"

"Oh, no ma'am. I wouldn't have allowed that."

"What about several days before?"

"No." He paused. "Wait. I guess I forgot about it." Chad ran his hand through his thick blond hair. "A few days before that reporter went missing, a guy stopped by to see if we could board his horse. I told him Mrs. Tucker didn't take in boarders."

"What made you remember him now?"

Chad shrugged. "We get folks stopping in from time to time looking to board horses. But you can tell they know what they're talking about. I probably wouldn't have remembered this guy, but it was clear he had no knowledge of horses. Besides, I guess it's like you said. I put that box in the back of the closet after he left and forgot it was there."

"Was there anything unusual about him?"

"Like I said, he didn't know a thing about horses. When

I asked him what kind of horse he had, he couldn't tell me. And his shoes. They were banker shoes. You know tie ups, shiny. I've never seen a horse person dressed like a banker. But then, I guess some bankers have horses. Seems like they'd have someone else checking out stables for them though."

Enid scribbled in her reporter's notepad, the same kind Mia's abductor sent to the newspaper office. "Can you describe him?"

Chad rubbed his chin. "Probably mid-thirties. Light brown hair. He had on sunglasses, so I didn't see his eyes."

"How tall?"

"About my height, less than six feet. He looked like he worked out. I could see his biceps through his sweater." Chad was silent and appeared to be thinking. "Oh, and he had a tattoo on his arm. I saw it when he pushed his sleeve up."

Enid scribbled more notes.

"It was like claws. No, wait. Let me think. It was one claw."

Turning to a fresh page in her notepad, she pushed it toward Chad. "Can you draw it for me?"

He took her pen and sketched the tattoo.

She stiffened when she saw what he had drawn. "That's a bird's claw. A talon."

"Ma'am, are you okay? You look upset."

Enid's mind was swirling. "Yes, I'm sorry. I was just thinking. You need to tell Agent Carlson everything you've told me. But please don't tell him we've talked. Just tell him you were thinking about that day and remembered something he ought to know."

Chad smiled, seeming to enjoy their secret. "No, ma'am.

I won't tell him you were here."

"Did he come back again, this man? Did you ever see him again?"

"No, just that one time."

"What about when Mia, the reporter from our paper talked to you? Did you see anything unusual then?"

"Not as I recall. She asked me if I knew anything or had seen anyone, but I didn't remember this guy then, so I said no."

"Did you see Mia leave the stable area?"

"Like I told Agent Carlson and the FBI guy whose name I can't ever remember, I was busy tending the horses inside the barn when we talked. When we finished, she walked out of the barn to leave and that's all I saw."

"And this was a couple of days after Winnie was taken, is that right?"

"Yes, ma'am."

CHAPTER 34

When Enid and Josh returned to her house, she put the kettle on the stove. "You look like you need something stronger than tea," Josh said, walking to the refrigerator. "There's a couple glasses of Chardonnay left." He held the half-full bottle out toward her. "Interested?"

"Why not?" Enid walked to the living room sofa and sat, kicking off her shoes.

Josh handed her a glass of wine and sat beside her. "Ready to tell me what's got you rattled?"

She sipped the wine and set the glass down on the coffee table. "He was there. Talon."

Josh turned to face her. "What do you mean? The kidnapper?"

"About a week before Winnie was taken, he talked to their stable manager about boarding a horse."

"But how do you know it was him?"

"Chad said the man had a tattoo." She handed him her notepad, open to Chad's drawing. "He drew this. It's a talon."

"Could Chad describe the man?"

Enid repeated what Chad told her. "I know what you're thinking. Could it be the man at Sarah's you talked to? The description could match him, but also hundreds of other men around here." Her cell phone rang. "Hang on, let me get this. It's Cade." She took her wine glass with her to the kitchen to take the call.

"Cade, what a surprise."

"Sorry, luv, it's Olivia. Cade asked me to call you. He's in a meeting."

"Oh. I'm sure he's busy these days, between the new job and planning a wedding."

"Right-o. He's got a buggy full of work, that's for sure. Anyway, he . . . Wait, let me look at my note." The sound of paper shuffling. "Oh, here it is. He said there was a mate at university who always wanted to work with you. He had a crush on you, Cade thought."

"I vaguely remember someone like that. But what made Cade think of him?"

"Dunno, luv. I'm just the messenger."

"Did Cade remember his name?"

"No, but he said he shared a byline with you on an article about the return on investment, or lack of it, for acquiring a journalism degree."

Enid laughed. "I was pretty idealistic back then. But I do remember that article. Did Cade say anything else?"

"No, luv. That's it. He said to tell you to be careful."

"Of course. Thanks for calling, Olivia. Tell Cade . . . never mind. Thanks."

Enid swallowed the last bit of wine and took her glass back to the kitchen. Josh was sitting at the small dining table looking at some papers. "Cade okay?" he asked, looking up.

"It was his research assistant, Olivia." She relayed the conversation to Josh. "I'll see if I can find that article somewhere, but I may not have kept it." She looked at the papers on the table. "What's all that?"

Josh stood and took her hand, leading her back to the living room sofa. "There's something I want to discuss with you."

Enid sat beside Josh. "This sounds serious. Should I be concerned?"

"That depends on how you feel about private investigators."

"Are you thinking of hiring one?"

Josh laughed. "No, silly. I'm going to apply for a license."

"To be a PI? You?"

"Joshua Hart, Private Investigator. Don't you think that has a ring to it?"

"Don't you think that's a bit of a cliche? Ex-cop becomes a private detective. Maybe you could get your own TV show."

"Very funny. I'm being serious. I could get a license pretty quick with my background. Whit Carlson said he could help me get my application fast-tracked."

"Where did this come from, I mean your wanting to become a PI?"

"I've been thinking about how I could use my law enforcement background. Being a rent-a-cop doesn't have much appeal, so I decided this might be a better option. Of course, I could always drive a forklift at the distribution center, like we talked about."

Enid rubbed her temples with her fingers. "Where would you work? I mean, I imagine there's not much demand around here."

Josh pulled her close and held her. "We'll figure that out. There's demand in Columbia, Greenville, Charleston—any of those places."

Enid looked up and kissed him. "I like it that you said 'we'll figure it out.' If that's what you want to do, then I'm onboard."

Josh pushed her away gently and smiled. "So you think I'm a cliche, huh?"

CHAPTER 35

Enid looked through the cardboard bankers boxes retrieved from her attic. Only a few of them contained items and mementos from her university years: a few well-wishing notes from fellow students, some yellowed photos, and other miscellaneous items that once seemed valuable enough to save. But no copies of articles she had written for the university's student newspaper, the *Daily Gamecock*. She put the covers back on and shoved the boxes to the back of her closet, with a vow to go through them and get rid of most of the items she had been dragging around with her for years.

Next, she looked through the PDF collection of articles Talon had sent her but couldn't find a copy of the article Cade remembered. She then looked on her computer's hard drive for copies of old stories she had written in school but found nothing. Had she even kept copies of those early articles? If she had, they were likely on a memory stick stashed away somewhere or even more likely, discarded years ago. She went into her home office where her computer sat on a small table by the window. A set of plastic drawers on wheels, the kind often used to store craft materials, sat next to it. She rummaged through each drawer until she found a flat plastic container near the bottom. It wasn't labeled, and she had been meaning to check its contents but just never got around to it. She remembered copying several articles off one of her old computers to save to disk. Maybe this was it.

She pulled the shiny silver disk from its container, but then remembered she had no optical drive on this laptop. Maybe Josh had one on his, but she had not seen his laptop since he returned to Madden. He used his iPad to check the news and email his sister. "Josh?" she called out. No answer. He was likely outside, where he preferred to be most of the time. She went to the back door and looked across the backyard. "Josh? Are you out here?" No response.

His pickup was usually parked in the neighbor's yard through the woods, so she couldn't tell if he had left. Although, he wouldn't leave her alone, not until they arrested this Talon guy.

Enid walked to the front of the house. Josh was nowhere to be seen. Now she was starting to worry. Where was he? She went through the house, room to room, to see if he had fallen asleep somewhere. An icy cold fear gripped her chest. She made sure the front and back doors were locked.

A ping in the otherwise silent house made her jump. It was the signal of a message coming through on her laptop. She ran back to her office and looked at the screen. It was a SecureDrop notification. Hands shaking, she logged onto the system and accessed a new message from Talon:

"I have something you might want. Meet me at the quarry at 8:00 pm and I might give it back. No police or you won't get your present."

Enid closed her laptop and tried to steady her breathing. Surely Josh would walk through the door any minute now and tease her for worrying so much. But ten minutes later, Josh was still missing. Grabbing her sweater, she ran out the back door and headed to the woods separating her from the neighbor's house. Out of breath by the time she got there, she stopped in her tracks when she saw Josh's pickup. If his truck was still here, then where was he?

Fear overcame her. Realizing she had taken Josh's protective presence for granted, she was now alone in the woods, with no one around to come to her aid. Maybe Talon wanted to lure her outside. She pulled her sweater closer and ran back toward her house.

Cursing herself for not locking the door behind her when she ran out, she checked all the rooms. It was nearly 4:00 now. She called Jack and left a message for him to call immediately.

When her cell rang, she assumed it was Jack. But then she realized it was her old cell phone ringing. "Jack?"

A male voice responded. "No, it's Ty."

"Ty?"

"Call me back on a secure line." The line went dead.

Before calling Ty, she went to the settings of her new phone and blocked her number from appearing when she called. Only her closest acquaintances had access to this new number. She jotted down Ty's number and called it on her burner phone.

"Thanks for calling me back," Ty said.

"What's this all about? What do you want?"

"I heard from Talon. He wants to set up a meeting with you, right?"

Could she trust Ty? How did he know what was going on? "Yes. But how are you involved?"

"You shouldn't go alone. Do you want me to go with you?"

Enid wanted to scream that she had no more reason to trust him than Talon. "Thanks, but I'll be fine."

"I know what's going on, so don't be stupid. I won't hurt

you." He paused. "I'm just after the story, that's all."

"I told you, I'll be fine." After the call ended, Enid stared at the cell phone. Her mind was racing, yet numb at the same time. When her burner phone rang, she jumped. Jack's image appeared on her screen. "Jack, I'm so glad you called. I need to talk to you. Now, if you can. Here, at my house."

• • •

"You've got to report Josh's disappearance to SLED. What's his buddy's name?" Jack asked.

"It's Whit Carlson, but I'm not going to risk Josh's life by getting them involved."

Jack took Enid's hands in his. "And I'm not going to let you go off with some whacked up reporter to meet a killer. No, it's not going to happen."

In a torrent of emotion, Enid screamed and cried at the same time. "Why me? What have I done to this guy Talon to make him torment me?"

"Not that this will make you feel better, but I think he's in love with you, in his own sick way. He's obsessed with getting close to you. And remember when he first contacted you, he said he wanted to make you famous?"

Enid wiped her eyes with her sleeve and nodded.

"If you upset him in any way, he'll turn on you for not returning his affection. You cannot meet with him alone."

"But you know how law enforcement works. Their primary objective is to catch this guy, and if there's collateral damage, that's just too bad. My objective is to get Josh back safely, and hopefully Winnie too."

"Have you called Josh's cell phone?"

"At least ten times. It goes directly to voice mail."

Sitting side by side with Jack on the sofa in her living room, Enid rested her head on his shoulder. "What will I do if something happens to Josh? It will be my fault."

Jack gently pulled her away so he could look at her. "Stop it. This is not your fault." He took a deep breath. "For the record, I think this is an incredibly bad idea. But I'll go with you and hide in the back seat."

Enid sat up abruptly. "No, I can't put you in danger too. No. If this guy's obsessed with me, he won't hurt me."

"Need I remind you this guy is crazy, so he may not follow your logic. Worse case, he'll try to kidnap you too. I will tie you up in this house if I have to, to keep you from going alone." Jack tapped a number on his cell phone. "Ginger, it's me. I won't be back in the office today. Hold down the fort for me." He listened for a moment. "Well, tell Mr. Wonderful he'll have to come back later. I'm unavailable." He punched the red button emphatically to end the call. "That guy is beginning to get on my nerves."

"Who are you talking about?"

"Darren Smoak, or Mr. Wonderful, as Ginger calls him."

"I miss working in the office with her," Enid said.

"You can always come back, at least as long as I still own the place."

"I can't until all this is resolved. We've got some time before we leave, so if you need to go back in or do some work, don't worry. I won't run out the door and leave you." She kissed Jack on the cheek. "You are the best friend a girl could ask for."

Jack blushed. "Yeah, yeah. That's me. Now let's get a game plan together."

CHAPTER 36

With a few hours to kill, Jack got his laptop from the car and set it up on Enid's dining table to work. "I'll just catch up on a few things here, and I'll stay out of your way. That is, unless you need me to help take your mind off, well, you know, everything that's happening."

"That's sweet of you, but I'm going to look for an article Cade mentioned. Some guy I shared a byline with in college apparently had a big crush on me. I barely remember him, but Cade thinks I should check it out."

"Sounds like it's worth looking into, but it's probably nothing. If you're sure you're OK, I might rest a bit on your sofa instead of pretending to work."

"Are you feeling alright?"

"Yeah, just a little tired. I think the stress of getting all the paperwork together for the contract is wearing me down."

"Does it look like it's going through?"

"My attorney says there're still a couple things he wants to check into. The sooner this is all behind me, the better."

"Well, you rest, and I'll look for that article." Enid settled down at the desk in her office, but she couldn't stop thinking of Josh. She tried to remind herself he was a trained law enforcement professional and even if Talon had taken him, Josh would find a way to save himself. That is, if he was taken. Josh was always so observant about his surroundings.

None of it made sense. Unless it was someone he knew. That's the only way he would have let someone get close enough to overtake him.

She made herself focus on the task at hand. Maybe Jack's laptop had an optical drive that would read the CD she found. She walked to the living room. Jack's eyes were closed. She had a feeling he wasn't telling her everything about his health. She walked softly into the kitchen. Luckily, this was Jack's older laptop and had a CD drive. She slid the silver disk into the slot and waited while the whirring sound went on for what seemed like forever. Finally, a long list of files appeared on the screen. She clicked on each one, checking the bylines or any mention of the ROI of college tuition. About halfway through the list, she was ready to give up. The article Cade mentioned just wasn't here—if it existed at all. Maybe his memory was faulty. Glancing at the computer clock, she had plenty of time to finish checking the list, so she tiptoed back to her office and got a USB drive to capture the articles from the CD.

After opening the files on her own laptop, she saw a small file near the bottom of the list. When she clicked on it, an article appeared on the screen: "Is Your Journalism Degree a Good Investment?" It was written by Enid Morgan, her maiden name, and Marcus A. Cooper. She skimmed the article and it appeared to be the one Cade mentioned. But who was Marcus Cooper? She closed her eyes and tried to remember working with him, but no image came to mind.

Typing his name into Google, she hoped to find a photo or something that would jog her memory. Unfortunately, she did not find a match for someone who would be about her age. A few obituaries came up, but most of these men were too old to have been in school with her. She also checked Facebook and Twitter. A long list of Marcus Coopers came up. She scanned the photos of each and tried to find someone about her age that might jog her memory. But with no luck. Same with Twitter.

After an hour of looking in WhitePages.com and other places, she gave up. The newspaper had other search resources she would have to use to dig deeper, but it was getting late. She and Jack needed to get on the road, as the quarry was nearly an hour away. Talon didn't have to say which quarry. There was only one around here that locals referred to as "the quarry." It was an abandoned, open-pit quartz mine, alleged to be haunted. Was Talon a local? Is that why he made the reference so casually with the assumption she'd know where to meet him?

She closed her laptop and went to her bedroom to get the 9 mm gun Cade gave her when they were married and then made sure she had her concealed permit in her tote, not that it would matter in this situation. She had shot someone fatally a few years back when she was helping the local inn owner look for his missing daughter, and she hoped she would never have to use a gun again. She tried to block out those painful memories and refocus on Josh. If they both lived through this ordeal, they needed to talk about their future together. She blinked back the tears. No time for emotions now.

"Hey, you ready to leave?" Jack asked.

Startled, Enid turned to him. "I didn't know you were awake. Yes, let's go."

Jack nodded. "If Josh were here, he'd say, 'lock and load.'"

CHAPTER 37

Enid glanced at the time on her car radio. It was five minutes before 8:00 pm and they still had a few miles to go. As soon as she increased her speed, she hit a pothole in the road. "Sorry about that. You okay back there?"

"Yeah, a few bruises but otherwise okay," Jack said. "Try not to kill me before we get there."

"What do you know about the quarry?"

"Not much, mostly tall tales. There have been several drownings there. Most were teenagers. It's been closed for a long time. By the way, there are 'no trespassing' signs everywhere, so there may be surveillance cameras too."

"This guy's too smart to get caught on camera. You can rest assured he's disabled them if there were any."

"True."

"There's the entrance. Stay down and cover yourself."

"What do you see?" Jack's voice was muffled under the blanket.

"There's a metal gate and it seems to be partially open. I guess that's Talon's welcome mat for me. I'm going to get out and open it the rest of the way." Enid left the car running and looked around. All she could see was darkness. Off in the distance in the quarry, a mercury vapor light on a tall pole cast shadows on the stone walls, partially illuminating the deep, dark water below. A whip-poor-will called out in the distance. She switched on the LED flashlight and shone it past the gate. There was a narrow dirt road that disappeared into the darkness.

Under the pretense of getting her jacket in case Talon was watching her, she went back to the car. She grabbed her jacket on the front seat and whispered to Jack. "The road is narrow and not well lit. I'm going to walk in. If I don't come back, you know what to do."

She put her jacket on and aimed the light at the dirt road to avoid stepping in a hole. All she needed now was a twisted ankle. *Please, God, let Josh be safe.*

The road circled the perimeter of the quarry. The drop was at least fifty feet to the water. No wonder teenagers got killed jumping from the ledges. She shivered and pulled her jacket closer. And then she stopped in her tracks. A red laser beam was focused on her flashlight. The beam then focused on the ground in front of her. What did he want? Again, the beam zeroed in on her flashlight and then the ground. He must want her to put the light down. She left it on and laid it on the ground in front of her. The red beam then focused on the switch on the handle. He wanted her to turn off the light, so she did. Suddenly, the mercury vapor light went dark. She was now in total darkness on a cloudy night.

"Well, I must admit, I'm surprised you came to see me." The mechanically altered voice sounded even more eerie in the darkness.

"I'm here, just like you asked. Where is Josh?"

A crude laugh pierced the night. "You mean that man of yours who was supposed to protect you? He couldn't even protect himself. Did you really think I'd let him come between us?"

"Just let him go, and I'll do whatever you want. It's me you're after, not Josh."

"By the way, I've made arrangements with Ty to write the stories about you. He'll be sure to say how brave you are. And how loyal you are to your friends. I told you I'd make you famous. Just work with him. If you don't, well, things could get messy. I don't like messy, do you?"

"I'll work with Ty. Now please, let Josh go."

"Keep the light off until you've counted to sixty slowly. Then you can turn it on. We wouldn't want you to fall into the quarry accidentally. I understand there are already several ghosts here."

"But . . ." Enid's heart was pounding. "Please," she whispered. Tears streamed down her cheeks as she counted. "One, two, three, four, five . . ." After what seemed like an eternity, she finally got to sixty and reached down to grab the flashlight. With trembling hands, she managed to turn it on. She surveyed the area around her by shining the light in a circular arc but couldn't see anything. Was Talon just playing with her? Where was Josh?

"Hello. Is anybody there?" Enid called out. She stepped a few feet forward. Suddenly the mercury vapor lights came on again. What was that propped against the granite wall? She walked toward whatever was covered in a blue painter's tarp. *Oh, God, no. Don't let him be dead.*

"Josh?" She pulled the tarp open and gasped. "Oh, God. Are you alright?"

A voice sobbed, "Yes, ma'am."

Enid pulled off the duct tape from Winnie's wrists. "You're safe now. You're going home."

Once she had freed Winnie's hands, the girl grabbed Enid around the neck and wouldn't let go. She was sobbing uncontrollably. "I want my momma. Please take me home."

Enid wiped the tears from her own face and took

Winnie's hand. "Can you walk?"

Winnie held her hand tightly. "Yes, ma'am."

CHAPTER 38

Enid opened the passenger door of her car. "Jack, it's me. And I've got Winnie." She helped Winnie inside. "A friend is in the back seat. He won't hurt you. He's here to protect us." She saw Jack's head pop up from under the blanket. "No, get down. We don't know if he's still watching. We're fine. I'm going to get us out of here and fill you in after we're safe."

"What about Josh?" Jack asked.

"No sign of him. It was another of Talon's tricks."

When Enid was sure they weren't being followed, she said, "Jack, you can sit up now. I think we're safe."

Jack tossed the blanket to one side and sat on the seat. "Is that really Winnie?"

Enid caressed Winnie's hair and smiled. "Yes, it is. Let's get this young lady home to her mother."

Jack pulled his cell phone from his pocket. "I'm calling her now so Mrs. Tucker can call SLED and the FBI. They're not going to be happy with us."

Enid dreaded the inevitable admonishment that was sure to come once the celebration ended. The authorities wouldn't be happy about her meeting Talon without their knowledge. But Winnie was going home, and that's what mattered. Her thoughts kept going back to Josh. Maybe Talon didn't have him. But Josh wouldn't leave without telling her.

When Jack called Mrs. Tucker, she thought it was a prank call. He handed the phone to Winnie. "Tell your mother you're safe."

Winnie took the phone from Jack and put it to her ear, hesitating briefly. "Mama? It's me. Winnie."

Enid could hear Mrs. Tucker screaming in joy. Whatever SLED and the FBI did to her, that moment was worth it.

Less than an hour later, Enid pulled into the Tucker's driveway behind a SLED car and two black vehicles.

As soon as the car stopped, Winnie jumped out of the car and ran toward the house. She was nearly to the front porch when Mrs. Tucker came running out the door. "Winnie, oh God! It's really you. Are you okay?" She held Winnie close until Winnie gently pulled away.

"I'm alright, Momma. Really."

Mrs. Tucker put her hand on her heart and looked at Enid. "Thank you." She then said to Winnie. "Come on, honey, let's go inside."

Enid watched as mother and daughter held hands and walked into the house.

Jack started toward Carlson and motioned for Enid to follow. "Come on. Let's get this over with."

"No, I pulled you into this. It's my problem. Get in the car."

"But . . ." Jack looked at Carlson. "She's been through a lot too. Take it easy."

Agent Carlson walked toward Enid. "I'm not sure whether to have you arrested for obstruction and withholding information in a kidnapping case, or to recommend you for a medal. What were you thinking?"

"Josh is missing. He disappeared from my place earlier today. I thought I was going to get him back. I had no idea it would be Winnie."

"Why didn't you notify us immediately?"

Enid pushed her shoulders back when she realized she had been slumping under the weight of worry. "I'm ready to give you a statement. Do you want to do it here or at my place?"

"Let me go inside and tell them where I'll be, and then I'll come to your house. They'll be talking with Miss Tucker for several hours. She may remember something that would help us find this bastard. And I need to put out a search for Josh."

"No, don't do that until I can talk with you."

Enid forced herself to hold back tears of exhaustion, fear for Josh's safety, and the joy of seeing Winnie home again.

"I can't promise that. Just go to your house," Carlson said. "I'll be there as soon as I can."

Enid nodded. As she turned to walk back to her car, Carlson called out to her. "Off the record, I'm proud of you. You did a good, although stupid, thing. But I'll deny I ever said it."

CHAPTER 39

It was nearly 2:00 am by the time Agent Carlson sat across from her at the dining table. Jack was asleep on the living room sofa. "I'm sure you realize that time is of the essence here," Carlson said. "Tell me everything you know or remember about Josh's disappearance."

Enid sipped her tea, which was now only lukewarm. "I was looking through a box of old college papers. When I'm busy or working, Josh usually hangs around outside even if it's just on the porch." She blinked back tears. "You know how he loves being outside."

Carlson nodded. "Yes, that's Josh, for sure. Go on."

"When I finished and started looking for him, he just wasn't here. I ran through the woods to the neighbor's yard where Josh parks his pickup, and it was there."

"So why didn't you call me then?"

Enid handed him a printout of the message from Talon. "Because I got this message through SecureDrop. I thought he had Josh. If I had known it was Winnie, I would have called you."

"Surely I don't have to tell you that you can't trust this guy Talon. He's already killed at least one person that we know of. And if he's obsessed with you, he may take out his jealousy on Josh."

"I thought of that too. At least we have Winnie back safely. I'm thankful she doesn't seem to be hurt, but I'm also confused. Was she just a pawn in his sick game?"

"Who knows? For now, we'll just have to be grateful for a good outcome."

Carlson's cell phone rang. "I'll be right back. I need to take this." He walked into the hall bath and shut the door, returning a few minutes later. "Sorry for the interruption. That was my FBI contact. They asked Winnie if she knew anything about Josh or anyone else Talon might be holding. Unfortunately, she did not. In fact, she said Talon was kind to her and kept assuring her she would be alright and would see her mother soon."

"That just reinforces that Winnie was only taken to up the ante."

"We can't dismiss the possibility that Josh was the intended victim all along."

"How could that be? Josh was in New Mexico when all this started." Before Carlson could respond, she added, "But of course, if he was targeting Josh, he could have easily learned of his connection to Madden and to me. Maybe Talon's obsession with me is just a ruse." She rubbed her temples. "I can't think anymore. Just please don't push this guy and put Josh in even more danger."

"We won't. The FBI is running a profile on Talon. Maybe that will give us something to go on. And I'll get a guy out here to check around for any clues. He'll be dressed as someone doing yard work for you. In the meantime—"

"I know, call you if anything happens. Just please help me find Josh."

When Carlson shut the front door, Jack sat up on the sofa. "Sorry I fell asleep. Did I miss the party?"

Enid sat on the sofa beside him. "You look pale. Are you withholding something you need to tell me? I couldn't take it if anything happened to you too."

"I smell coffee. Get me a cup and I'll fill you in."

· · ·

Jack sat at Enid's dining table, in the same seat Agent Carlson had occupied earlier. "Did you make this coffee?"

"I made it for Carlson, but he didn't drink any. Why?"

"Just proves you should never let a tea drinker make coffee. But I probably need it this strong right now."

"Sorry. Josh usually makes his own coffee."

Jack put his hand on hers. "It's perfect. Now tell me what Carlson said."

Enid filled Jack in on her conversation with the SLED agent as Jack took small sips of coffee.

"It never occurred to me that Josh could have been the target all along. I guess we'll just have to keep an open mind." He patted her hand. "We'll get him back. Josh is smart, strong, and resourceful. He can take care of himself."

Enid nodded. "I know everyone's doing their best. Now tell me about you. What's wrong?"

"I wasn't trying to withhold anything from you, but I knew you had a lot on your mind. I would have told you later."

"Told me what? Go on, please."

"You know my attorney, Randy, has been reviewing the contract for selling the paper to Darren."

"Has Randy found something wrong with the deal?"

"Maybe. Ordinarily, an attorney might not have checked the buyer's background so thoroughly. But Darren and Randy just didn't hit it off. In fact, they got into a pissing contest immediately. And since Randy is not just my attorney but also an old personal friend, he was determined to make sure Darren wasn't pulling anything over on me."

"And was he?"

"Well, here's where it gets interesting. The contract seems to be legit, but Darren has ties with some unsavory folks, at least according to Randy."

"Do you mean organized crime?"

"Not the Mafia or anything like that. These are more like international businessmen who appear legitimate on the surface but control a lot of money and people. Randy suspects they launder money through their international businesses and accounts."

Enid leaned back in her chair. "This is all too much for me to grasp. Then why would Darren want to buy a small local newspaper? When he shared his vision with me, it sounded like a solid, legitimate strategy."

"I don't know for sure, but Randy thinks the paper may be a cover and a way to send coded messages to his shady cronies. In fact, Randy says Darren owns another small paper in Colorado. He may want multiple papers to spread the messages around and avoid suspicion. Who knows?"

Enid threw back her head and laughed. "You can't be serious. This sounds like the plot of a badly written movie script." Jack didn't laugh with her. "But you're not kidding, are you? And Colorado is just above New Mexico, where Josh grew up."

"I don't have to tell you that we're living in Weird World these days, but let's not get carried away with conspiracy theories. I'm just telling you what Randy suspects. I don't know what I believe. But I do know Darren has changed from when I mentored him as a young reporter. Maybe he's telling the truth about his intentions for the paper."

"Want another cup of coffee?"

Jack smiled. "No thanks. I'd like to sleep sometime before next week."

"So what are you going to do? About selling the paper, I mean."

"Nothing right now. I'm stalling Darren while Randy does more digging. I'm a little concerned that Randy wants Darren to be guilty of something. I think Randy may have lost his objectivity. But I also don't want to hand this newspaper over to a crook, or worse. The paper has been around for a long time and has a good reputation. It deserves a worthy new owner." He stood up. "Mind if I sleep on your sofa tonight? I don't think I want to drive back to Madden this late."

"Of course. But use the futon in my office."

"Thanks. I hope you can get some sleep."

"Me too. I've got a lot to think about in the morning."

CHAPTER 40

Jack left early the next morning, and Enid sat alone at the table munching on a stale bagel with a generous slather of cream cheese. When her cell phone rang, she wasn't surprised to see Ty's name on the screen. "I figured you'd be calling. But I'm not going to give you an interview."

"I guess you haven't seen my story this morning."

"In the *State* newspaper?"

"Nah, I left 'em. They didn't appreciate my aggressive pursuit of the truth. But this story is going to increase my worth substantially in the job market. Just wait and see. Now I work for an online publication. I made a PDF to send you since it's only published on the dark web. I need to stay out of the spotlight until I get what I need from Talon. Hold a second." Almost immediately, a text from Ty popped up.

"I'll read it later," Enid said.

"You might want to look at it now."

"Alright, hold on." Enid clicked on the PDF file and a short article appeared. As she read it, she could feel the energy draining from her body. "You can't print this."

"As you can see, I already have. I just need for you to confirm former Bowman County Sheriff Joshua Hart is missing."

"I can't do that. You're putting Josh's life at stake. How could you?"

"Read the rest of it before you condemn me."

Enid read further. Ty had lavishly praised her heroism and bravery in rescuing Winifred Tucker. "First of all, where did you get this information? And why do you keep pulling me into it?"

"Trust me, I'd prefer not to praise another reporter, but that's the agreement I have with Talon."

"Agreement? What agreement? What have you done?"

"What I've done is what you would have done. In fact, what you've done in the past. I do whatever it takes to get the story. Remember, he reached out to me after you wouldn't play nice." Ty laughed. "That guy is totally, I mean totally, infatuated with you."

Lack of sleep, mental fatigue, and stress washed over Enid. "If you cause Talon to hurt Josh, I will personally come after you. And when I pursued those stories, it was to help the victims, not to build my reputation."

"Aw, that's sweet. And that's exactly what Talon said about you. Like I said, that guy worships you."

Enid took a few deep breaths to calm herself. "Alright, here's the deal. You give me what I need, and I'll confirm Josh's disappearance." Enid convinced herself she wasn't giving up much, since Ty had already printed the information as a "rumor," and so far at least, the article was only in an underground publication. But now she was worried more than ever about Josh's safety.

"Josh is not here, but there's no evidence of foul play," she said. "He may have been called away on an emergency. After all, we're not married, and he doesn't report to me."

"But he's hired by Bowman County to protect you."

Where did he get his information? Did Ty have connections in law enforcement? That wouldn't be unusual, given that he previously worked for one of the state's largest newspapers. "I cannot confirm or deny that information," she said.

"And here I thought you wanted to play fair."

"Dammit, Ty. This isn't a game. If I let you publicize that Josh is not here, then I'm inviting Talon or anyone else to come after me."

"Fair enough. But just for the record, I don't think Talon wants to hurt you. He's just obsessed."

"Well, your mister nice guy killed one of our reporters. Have you forgotten that?"

"He said she tried to attack him."

"So he taunted me by sending her notebook and luring SLED to where her body was located? And don't forget he sent Winnie's bracelet to me just to rattle me."

"Alright, we won't print anything about Josh being hired to protect you. I don't know if Talon knows that, but he's probably figured it out. The guy's not stupid."

"Has Talon said anything about how he knows me? He sent me a collection of my articles going all the way back to my years at the university."

"He just told me he's admired you for a long time and has been following your career. He said when you left journalism and went to work at the bank in Charlotte, he was devastated. Waste of your talent, he said. And that's all I know. Seriously."

Enid wasn't sure if she believed Ty. "One more question. Do you know anyone named Seth who works for the distribution center outside of Madden?"

"Now that's a random question. Why would I?"

"And what about Darren Smoak?"

Ty waited what seemed a long time to reply. "What's he got to do with any of this?"

Enid sat up in her chair. "Do you know him? Or has Talon mentioned him?" Her heart was pounding.

"No, I don't know him personally, if that's what you're asking."

"But you've heard of him, right?"

"He's one of the three guys who started this underground paper I work for, the *Nosy Rag*."

Enid was furiously jotting notes. "What else do you know about him? Have you heard anyone else talking about Smoak?"

"Whoa. We're outside our agreement now. If you want answers, you've got to pony up some serious info. Do you think Smoak's involved with Talon?"

Until this moment, the idea would have been unthinkable. But now, anything was possible and anyone could be involved. "He's buying our newspaper, or trying to. I was just curious since you obviously have connections."

"Well, thanks for trying to flatter me, but I'm just a schmuck trying to sell stories. Kinda like you."

Enid let that comment go without response. "If you hear anything about Josh, let me know immediately."

"Gotta go." With that final comment, the call ended.

Should she tell Agent Carlson about this conversation with Ty? If she were still working for the *Tri-County Gazette*, she would be ethically obligated to do so to protect the paper. But she was a freelancer, much like Ty, though she hated to admit it. Right now, Ty was her only connection to Talon. And even though she didn't know for sure that he had Josh, she couldn't imagine another scenario in which Josh would have abandoned her.

CHAPTER 41

Before calling Jack, Enid made a few more notes about her conversation with Ty. Talking with him made her feel naïve and vulnerable. Was Darren involved somehow? She texted Jack and asked him if they could meet at Sarah's so she could fill him in on what she had learned. She was starting to get cabin fever from staying in the house so much. Agent Carlson promised to have someone else assigned to cover her, and when she peeped between the front window blinds, a black sedan was parked in her driveway.

About thirty minutes later, she walked out the door, waving to the guy in the black car, who just nodded an acknowledgment. Having someone to protect her was comforting in some respects, but she valued her privacy. Having a stranger hanging around was invasive.

The drive to Madden took about twenty minutes. Jack would have walked from the newspaper office, so his pickup wouldn't be on the street. Hoping he would already be inside, she walked into Sarah's and scanned the occupants. Her admirer was not there, and her usual booth was open. The waitperson nodded for her to take the seat.

"Here you go, hon. A nice, piping hot Earl Grey, just for you. Want some whole grain toast to go with that?"

"That would be nice, thanks. Jack is joining me, so you might as well bring a cup of coffee too."

"It's nice to have you back in your usual spot. That

creepy guy hasn't been in for a while."

"That's good." Enid saw Jack walk in and motioned for him to join her.

"Hey. Your text worried me. Is everything okay?"

Enid waited for Jack to get his coffee and then told him about her conversation with Ty, leaving out the part about Darren.

"Have you told SLED yet?"

Enid stared at her teacup. "I'm not planning to tell Whit. Not yet."

Jack pushed back slightly from the table. "This is a dangerous game you're playing with Ty, not to mention probably illegal."

Enid leaned in and spoke softly. "If I shut down my only way of communicating with Talon, then I might never see Josh again. That's not an option. Agent Carlson said SLED is trying to find Josh, and Carlson knows about Ty from our previous conversations. I'm not a suspect. Why do I have to report every conversation?"

"You're trying awfully hard to convince yourself. And now you've made me an accomplice to your scheme." Jack put another pack of sugar in his coffee. "So what do you want me to do?"

"There's more to my conversation with Ty I haven't told you."

Jack laughed. "This just keeps getting better and better. Now what?"

"Ty left the *State* newspaper. He said they didn't approve of his 'aggressive pursuit of the truth,' even though they appreciated his exclusive coverage. Ty now works for an underground newspaper, the *Nosy Rag*. He says they only publish on the dark web." When she saw that Jack was about to interrupt, she held up her hand. "Wait, let me finish. Ty says three guys started the paper." She paused. "One of the guys is Darren Smoak."

Jack nearly choked on his coffee. "Darren? Are you serious?"

"That's what Ty said. I don't know why he would have any reason to lie. I'm the one who asked him if he knew Darren. I just thought maybe Ty had some dirt on Darren that might help your attorney investigate him. I had no idea of Darren's involvement with the underground paper."

"Well, I'd say that's some pretty serious dirt. These underground papers don't have to adhere to any standards, so they can publish what they want, true or not. Some are also used by extremist groups for communicating in code language. It's scary stuff." Jack shook his head. "What's happened to journalism? The world we knew is dying before our very eyes."

"I agree, but I think you're missing something. If Ty is in contact with Talon, and Ty works for Darren and these other two guys, then there's a possibility Darren and Talon are connected."

Jack rubbed his neck. "I need to talk to Randy. But let's not jump to conclusions here. And I still think you need to talk to Agent Carlson."

"You have a Hold Harmless Agreement from me. I'm not an employee any longer, so whatever happens, you can disavow any knowledge or involvement."

Jack put his hand on Enid's. "My dear, dear friend. Do you not realize by now that I would do anything to protect you? I'm not going to walk away." He withdrew his hand. "But I do worry. Let's see what we can find out the next couple of days. And then we need to revisit this conversation. Agreed?"

Enid nodded. "I was thinking. Ginger is not only a great, although sometimes annoying, office manager, but she is also an outstanding researcher. The newspaper has more re-sources than I do as an independent contractor. How do you feel about letting her help me?"

"I don't know anything about this conversation, and I'll tell her I don't know anything. I'll leave it to her if she wants to get involved. Understand?"

Enid smiled. "You know she'll jump all over this."

"I know." Jack put a five-dollar bill on the table and stood to leave.

CHAPTER 42

When Enid left Sarah's, she saw the black vehicle parked on the street. He wasn't inconspicuous, but that was probably the point. She walked across the street and down a few doors to the newspaper office. Glancing over her shoulder, the guy from the black car was walking on the opposite side of the street in the same direction she was going. She would never be able to shake him off if she needed to. But Jack was right. This was no game and she had no intentions of playing GI Jane, although she was on a mission to get Josh back safely.

She glanced around the parking lot beside the old red brick building. Jack's pickup was in its usual spot, and Ginger's car was next to it.

When Enid walked inside, she wasn't prepared for Ginger's reaction. She ran to Enid and gave her a hug. "I've missed you. Jack said Winnie Tucker is back home and that you got her back. That's so awesome."

"Well, thanks, but I don't deserve any credit. I guess Jack told you about Josh."

Ginger shook her head. "He did. I'm so sorry. I mean I'm not assuming anything bad has happened, but I'm sorry he's not with you. You guys are such a cute couple. I hope I find a man like Josh one day."

"Look, I need to ask you about something, but now I'm beginning to ask myself if this is a good idea."

Ginger put her hand on Enid's arm and lowered her voice. "Jack told me you needed my help, and it was up to me to agree or not. He didn't say what it was about, other than he didn't want to know anything about it. So, of course, I'll help you."

Enid motioned down the hallway. "Can we meet in the conference room? I don't want anyone to walk in and see us talking."

"Sure. I can catch any calls from the phone in there."

When they were settled at the worn wooden table that had been in the newspaper office for decades, Enid began filling Ginger in on all that had happened.

"Wow. That's so cool. I don't mean the murder or the kidnapping. I just mean . . . Actually, I'm not sure what I mean, so go on."

"Jack doesn't want to know about any of this. And if I get caught meddling in this investigation, you could be in trouble. I know you love to dig up stuff and do research, but this is serious, so you can say no, and I'll understand."

"Say no more, girl. I'm in. What do you need?"

Enid reached in her tote and retrieved a copy of the articles Talon had sent her. "This guy knows my work. Some of these articles go way back, and he couldn't have known about them unless he knew me at the university. Cade said there was a guy who did an article with me on the ROI of a journalism degree. I found a copy of it, but I barely remember doing it. If this guy Cade mentioned is who I kinda remember, he was seriously overweight and nerdy. You know, thick glasses, sloppy dresser. But then, I might be remembering someone else. I contacted the School of Journalism, but they didn't find anyone with the name Talon. Not that I thought he would use his real name."

"So you want me to help you find this guy?"

"Yes, but there's more." Enid told Ginger about Ty and his relationship with Darren Smoak.

Ginger slammed her palm on the table. "I knew it. I knew that creep was scum. I'll be more than happy to check that further."

"The *Nosy Rag* is on the dark web."

"No problem, my dear. I have Tor on my personal computer. Give me that article Ty published and I'll see what I can dig up." She rubbed her hands together. "Thank you for letting me help you. I won't let you down."

"I know you're interested in being a reporter yourself, and I know this is the kind of work you love to do. But be careful and don't leave a trace."

"Girl, I know how to cover my tracks." She smiled at Enid. "But thanks for your concern." Ginger stood. "I'm going to start on this right away. I'll keep you posted."

"Thanks. You're the best. And you're going to be a great investigative reporter one day."

CHAPTER 43

During the drive home, Enid decided it was time to force Talon's hand. He had already killed one person and would kill again—if he hadn't already. Maybe he was stringing her along just to stay close to her. When she got to her house, she opened her laptop in her home office, logged onto SecureDrop, and began typing: "Thank you for returning Winnifred Tucker unharmed, but I need to know about Josh. Do you have him? Is he alive? If you don't send me proof of life, I will shut down communication with you. Don't hurt him to get to me."

Before sending the message, she thought of her conversation with Agent Carlson. What if Josh had been Talon's target all along? She brushed those thoughts aside for now and hit send.

Writing had always been her way of focusing whenever her thoughts were all over the place, a condition one of her professors called "monkey mind." She reached for her legal pad and a pen to list the questions swirling around in her head.

- Did Talon take Josh?
- If so, why?
- Was Talon one of her classmates at college?
- If not, who else would have access to her articles from the college newspaper?
- Why would Darren start an underground newspa-

per?
- Why did Darren want to buy the *Tri-County Gazette* from Jack?
- Is Ty who he says he is?
- Is Seth, the guy from Sarah's, involved?

There was no point in asking why Talon was obsessed with her. She knew enough about stalking to know that often there was no logical reason—just some twisted perversion that made sense only to the stalker. Even though Ty said Talon admired her and wanted her to be recognized for her work, she also knew Talon could turn on her quickly. Maybe he was just jealous of Josh's involvement with her. She shuddered involuntarily at the idea that Talon might hurt or even kill Josh to eliminate the competition.

She put the list aside. Even though she didn't have answers now, at least she had somewhat cleared her mind by dumping it all on paper. Glancing at the notes on her desk, she reminded herself she still had work to do for the newspaper. She began outlining an article about things that had changed in Madden since the distribution center had brought in so many new people. The town was still split on whether growth was good for the town's future or if it portended doom. The merchants she interviewed for the article were pleased with the increased business but also mourned the loss of "old Madden."

A notification from SecureDrop popped up at the bottom of her screen. With her hands shaking, she accessed the message from Talon:

"I'm getting bored with your cowboy. He's alive but you'll just have to take my word for it. Remember, I make the rules, and I'm only doing this for your own good. I promised to make you famous, and I will."

Enid's stomach was in knots. Something wasn't right. Why wouldn't Talon give her proof Josh is alive? The likely answer was too heartbreaking to fathom.

After she cried all the tears she could, she went to the bathroom and washed her face. Now she was mad. Talon would not get away with killing Josh—or Mia. She would make sure of it.

Her ringing cell phone startled her out of her mental torture chamber. She wiped her eyes again and looked at the screen. It was Cade calling from London. Or maybe it was Olivia, his assistant. "Hello."

Cade's familiar voice was comforting. "Any word on Josh?"

Enid brought him up to date. "I don't feel good about this."

"I'm sorry. I know you love Josh, and I want you to be happy. So let's try not to jump to conclusions. This guy Talon sounds like a nutter, so I wouldn't try to figure him out. Maybe he's just playing head games with you."

"Thanks for trying to cheer me up. I hope SLED will figure out who this guy is. They've got an FBI profile on him, but I haven't seen it yet."

"Look, if you want to talk later, we can. But I just wanted to give you some information on that article I mentioned that you and that guy wrote in school. Amazingly, I found a digital copy in some old files from school. I can't believe I kept all of our articles. Anyway, you shared the byline with this guy Marcus A. Cooper. Do you remember him?"

"I found a copy too, but I don't remember much about him. Was he heavy and wore thick glasses? A nerdy looking guy?"

"If you're asking if he was fat and ugly, then yes, that's

him. He was smart, but annoying as all get out. He knew you and I were dating, but he kept trying to get you to go out with him."

"I must have done a pretty good job blocking him out, because I don't remember that."

"Anyway, I gotta run—we'll talk later."

After Cade's call, she opened the file containing the article she and Cooper had written and skimmed it again, hoping to job her memory. She was embarrassed at how bad her writing was back then. She could clearly tell which parts she and her co-author had written. She stared at the byline. Surely Marcus Cooper's infatuation had dissipated long ago.

She did a Google search but nothing came up on Marcus A. Cooper. If she knew what the "A" stood for as his middle name, she could narrow the search. But she certainly couldn't remember it, and it was doubtful she ever knew what it was. On a whim, she sent an email to Cade and asked him to have Olivia check the Associated Press list of employees to see if Marcus ever worked for them. Even if he was still in journalism, the odds of his working for the AP were slim, but she had nothing else to go on.

Next she used several background checking services she had access to. On the third try, she got a hit. Maybe, at least. Someone named Marcus Cooper worked for a small paper in North Carolina. Since she lived in Charlotte, North Carolina, prior to moving to Madden, the connection made her uneasy. But how many reporters named Marcus A. Cooper could there be in journalism? This Marcus's middle name was Alton. Marcus Alton Cooper. Since she didn't have a photo, she couldn't be sure if it was the same person she went to college with. And would she even recognize him? That was a more than a decade ago, and people change. She jotted down the name of the paper in North Carolina and then found the phone number on their website.

She placed the call and crossed her fingers they would give her some information. "Hi, this is Enid Blackwell in Madden, South Carolina. I work for the *Tri-County Gazette*. I've been looking for a friend of mine, Marcus A. Cooper. We went to school together, and I'd like to reconnect with him. I understand he works for you."

The woman on the other end replied, "I'll connect you with our office manager." The phone line was then filled with an annoying, way-too-loud version of "Close to You," an old Carpenters song.

Moments later, a male voice answered. "I understand you're looking for one of our employees. May I help you?"

Enid repeated the half-truth she had used earlier. "I'd really like to find Marcus. Could you help me?"

"I can't divulge any personal information, but I can tell you he doesn't work here any longer."

"Do you by any chance have a photo of him? I just want to make sure it's the same guy."

"I can send you a link to an article he did that shows his photo. That's public information."

"That would be great." Enid gave him her email address.

When the link came in and Enid clicked on it, an archived article from two years ago filled her screen. She stared at the photo, hoping she would recognize him. There was something about the eyes that looked familiar, but she couldn't be sure. The photo was black and white, so she couldn't tell his hair color, but it looked like a medium shade—not too dark or too light. But this guy was slim. He certainly wasn't heavy like the guy she remembered in college. People gain and lose weight all the time, but she couldn't be sure it was him.

Frustrated at another dead end, Enid made herself a cup of tea and studied her list of questions and notes to see if she had forgotten anything. She found herself subconsciously drawing a line under Alton, Marcus's middle name. While she stared at the name, she sipped her tea. And then nearly dropped her teacup.

As a child, she often played Scrabble with her cousins to pass the long summer days. After a while, they refused to play with her because she won all the time. One thing she learned from Scrabble was making anagrams.

Alton, its letters scrambled, was Talon.

After staring at her notepad for several minutes, she exhaled after realizing she had been holding her breath. Surely this was a coincidence. After all, many names had anagrams.

She enlarged the photo from the article and stared at it until her eyes watered. This photo wasn't the fat, nerdy guy she remembered. But was he Talon?

CHAPTER 44

The text message on Enid's phone was from Ginger. She wanted to meet with Enid and Jack that afternoon. Enid looked at the unfinished article on her desk and sighed. One thing she was loving about being a contractor is that no one cared how you dressed. In fact, it was expected that non-employees, who often made little money, would dress down, so Enid swapped out her sweatshirt for a sweater but kept the jeans and sneakers. She responded to Ginger that she was on the way and grabbed her tote.

On the drive to Madden, she called Agent Carlson and asked for an update. He said they had nothing to report. Or at least nothing he was willing to tell her. He assured her he would let her know immediately if they learned anything about Josh.

When she got to the newspaper office, Ginger and Jack were already in the small conference room. "I got here as fast as I could. What's up?" Jack was at the head of the table and Ginger was to his left. Enid sat across from her and took a notepad and pen from her tote.

"Ginger called this meeting, so I'll defer to her," Jack said.

"Okay, so here's the deal." She looked at Jack. "You didn't want to know about any of this, but this involves the man who is buying your, that is our, paper. So you need to know."

Jack nodded.

"What did you find?" Enid asked.

"Well, we already knew he wasn't a Boy Scout," Ginger said, glancing at Enid then to Jack. "Did he tell you he owned a couple of small-town newspapers?"

Jack shook his head. "No, he failed to mention that. Go on."

"Well, he's bought at least three local papers that I could find. He increased the digital subscriptions and then sold them to a consolidation company that builds a network of small newspapers."

"Nothing about that sounds illegal," Enid said.

"No, but he's had several lawsuits filed against him for not disclosing his intentions."

"In all fairness, he told me he planned to go all-digital," Jack said.

Ginger waved her notes in the air. "Wait, there's more. He also has several lawsuits pending against him from employees who didn't get paid."

"Whoa, now that's not good," Jack said. "You've given me enough already to talk with this guy. Anything else I should know?"

Ginger continued, "As you know, Darren is one of the three owners of the *Nosy Rag*, which is published underground only. There are no rules about the dark web, so he can't be held liable in the same way he can with legitimate newspapers. Now I don't have proof of any of this, but the word from one of my friends who spends a lot of time down under, you know, on the dark web, is that this newsletter trades in information that could be used for blackmailing people. The seller posts a news story with photos and information that could be damaging, and then bidders can buy that information and use it however they want to. Obviously, blackmail is the more profitable way to use it." She paused. "Keep in mind, that I can't prove this part. The part about buying up small papers I can substantiate, but not the rest. Besides, I wouldn't want to drag my friend into this."

"But why would Darren want to buy this or any local paper when he's clearly doing a more lucrative business with his underground paper?" Enid asked.

"That's a good question." Jack said. "One I intend to ask." He stood up. "Ginger, give me what you've got, and I'll talk to Darren." As Jack walked out of the conference room, he looked back and added, "He lied to me. That's not acceptable."

• • •

Less than an hour after his meeting with Ginger and Enid, Jack sat in the conference room with Darren. "You said you wanted to meet right away," Darren said. "I hope that means you've got a signed contract for me." He rubbed his hands together, grinning.

Jack massaged his neck. "Actually, I've called you here to tell you the deal is off. I'm no longer selling the paper. Not to you, anyway."

Darren sat up straight in his chair. "You can't do that. We had an agreement."

"No, we had a pending contract. And I'm not signing it." Jack took off his glasses and laid them on the table. "Tell me again why you wanted to buy this paper. There are plenty of others out there. You don't live in this community, and you're willing to cast aside our older readers who likely won't subscribe to an all-digital format. But what's more important is that you lied to me. You didn't disclose that you owned several small newspapers, some of which have sued you. And you also didn't tell me you co-publish an underground paper."

"But what does any of that matter? Besides, I'm paying you more than this little rag is worth. None of that other stuff has anything to do with our deal. And if you go back on our verbal agreement, I'll take you to court." He added, "You always were too much of an idealist."

"This little rag, as you called it, serves three counties of hardworking, honest folks who look to us to keep them informed by telling the truth. I don't know what kind of scheme you were planning on running with this paper as your front, but I won't permit it. If you want to sue me, go for it." Jack stood up. "Now get out of my newspaper office."

CHAPTER 45

After tossing all night, Enid woke up tired and cranky. All night long, she kept asking herself if she should talk to SLED about Marcus Alton Cooper and her suspicions. On one hand, they had the resources to track him down. On the other hand, if Cooper was Talon, he might kill Josh if he was cornered, assuming Josh was still alive.

Her head was throbbing as she made a cup of tea. What would Josh want her to do? She smiled. Ever the lawman, he would tell her to turn the bastard in and quit worrying about the consequences.

During the next hour, she picked up her phone twice to call Agent Carlson. What was stopping her, other than her worry about Josh? She read about people who could just sense if a loved one was still alive. It worried her that she didn't have that feeling. She didn't feel like Josh was dead or alive. She didn't feel anything other than sadness and an empty spot in her heart that he filled. They had been through so much, had fought off so many attacks on their alleged conflicts of interest: he as a law enforcement official and she as a local reporter in his jurisdiction. Now, all of that seemed so trivial. If Josh wanted to be a private detective, and she was no longer at the newspaper, they would be free to be together, without the shackles of their respective careers. But Josh was no longer here because some guy was obsessed with her. It wasn't fair, and she alternated between wanting to kill the guy and wanting to pull the covers over her head to escape. Neither option was acceptable.

"Third time's the charm," she said aloud as she tapped on Agent Carlson's cell number. He answered so quickly, it startled her. "Agent Carlson, this is—"

"What is it Ms. Blackwell. Are you alright?"

"Yes, I'm fine, thanks. But I need to talk to you as soon as possible. It's about Talon. I may know who he is."

"I'll be right there."

• • •

Less than an hour later, Agent Whit Carlson was sitting on Enid's living room sofa. "I would have been here sooner, but we've got another abduction reported."

"You don't think it's related, do you?"

"It looks more like a custody dispute kidnapping." He pulled out his notepad. "Now tell me what's going on. You said you might know who Talon is."

"Maybe. It's just a thought and I don't want to waste SLED's time or take you off in a wrong direction."

"Let me worry about that. Talk to me." His pen was poised on the notepad.

"Not too long ago, Talon sent me a file that had all of my old articles in it, including some from my college days when my ex-husband and I wrote for the student newsletter."

"Why didn't you tell me about this earlier? It could be important." He stared at Enid for what seemed like a long time. "Josh told me you had a tendency to go off on your own to investigate, but surely with Josh's life at stake, you're not doing that."

"If you're finished lecturing me, I'll continue. I wanted to find out what I could first."

"Go on, I'm listening."

"My ex, Cade Blackwell, is working in London now for the Associated Press. He reminded me about a guy at the University of South Carolina that shared a byline with me on an article. Cade had saved a copy of it. The guy's name is Marcus A. Cooper. I didn't remember the name and only vaguely remember his face."

"Why would Cade single this guy out?"

"Cade said the guy had a crush on me. I didn't realize it, or perhaps I just ignored it. As far as I know, Cooper and I wrote only the one article together." She pulled a copy of Cooper's photo from a manila folder and handed it to Carlson.

"I called one of his former employers and got a photo of someone named Marcus Alton Cooper." She pulled her doodle sheet from the folder and handed it to Carlson. "I don't recognize this guy. As I remember, the guy in college was heavy and wore thick glasses. Of course, I realize he could have lost weight and got contacts. I'm just saying, I cannot positively identify him. This may not even be the same guy. And I don't even know that Marcus Cooper sent those articles to me." She handed him the paper with the anagram scribbled on it.

Carlson looked at the note. "Interesting. But are you trying to tell me that because this guy's middle name also spells Talon that it might be him?"

"Look, I know it sounds crazy, but Talon has an insider's knowledge of journalism. He knows about SecureDrop. And he's fixated on my journalism career and has been in contact with Ty, the reporter I told you about that worked for the *State* newspaper."

Carlson's left eyebrow arched. "Are you still in contact with Talon?"

"We've only messaged a couple of times."

"Well, I think you're right. If he knows about SecureDrop, he's either a journalist or has been a confidential informant. And he knows law enforcement can't get to those messages."

Enid leaned forward. "Look, I want to be clear. I don't want you busting down his door and arresting him based on what I've told you. I could be wrong." She looked away briefly. "I just want Josh back safely."

"Ms. Blackwell, I think you've watched too much TV. If we find this guy and decide to arrest him, we'll have more than this conversation to go on, I assure you." He took out his phone and made photos of the papers Enid gave him and then handed them back to her. "Hold onto these. Is there anything else you haven't told me?"

"Nothing I know for sure."

Carlson threw back his head and laughed. "Sorry, it's just that Josh was right. What else is on your mind? Let me worry about proving it."

"It's just that, well, I wonder at times if Ty is involved. Or if Darren Smoak is tied up in this somehow."

"And Darren is . . .?"

"He's trying to buy the *Tri-County Gazette* from Jack Johnson." She continued to tell Carlson about the underground newspaper owned by Smoak that Ty now works for.

Carlson sat back against the sofa. "Wow. That's a lot of coincidences. But, on the other hand, this is a small town, and I wouldn't be surprised that many of you in journalism are connected somehow. But it's worth checking out. Before

Josh went missing, he told me about this guy Seth who works or worked for the distribution center. Josh said he confronted him. Have you seen Seth since?"

"No, he stopped coming to Sarah's after Josh talked to him." She paused. "Before you go, can you tell me about the FBI's profile of Talon?"

"Is this for you personally or an article?"

"I no longer work for the paper, although I am doing some freelance work for Jack. But I'm not writing an article about any of this. The *State* newspaper, the *Post and Courier*, and several other papers are all over it. Besides, Talon wants me to write about him, so I'm not going to for that reason alone." She sighed. "I'm worried sick about Josh, and maybe something you tell me about Talon's profile will jog my memory."

"Fair enough." He leaned forward slightly. "I know you and Josh are serious, and I can only imagine how worried you are. But I have to work with facts. The FBI says this guy is likely very intelligent, a loner, not married or with any close connections. Likely between thirty and forty years old. He's trying to make a name for himself, and his fixation on you may be just an excuse to prove himself. They feel he has, or had, a journalism background, or at least some knowledge and a strong interest in it. And they think he only took Winifred Tucker to get your attention. He's capable of killing, as we know from his killing Mia Olson, but he prefers only to taunt because it gives him power over people. He has narcissistic tendencies that make him want to control people and events." He pointed to the paper in Enid's hand. "If you're right about the anagram, this guy may like puzzles. I'll fill the FBI in on this."

"Is there anything else you aren't telling me?"

"No, but as you know, these stalkers can quickly turn on the person they are obsessed with. Just because he says he admires you doesn't mean he won't try to kill you too."

"I realize that. You said earlier that Josh may have been the intended target and that Talon may have gone after me to get to Josh. Do you still believe that?"

"I don't know anything at this point, but all cards are still on the table. If Josh was the target, and if Talon has him, as we assume, then the game may already be over."

CHAPTER 46

Josh glanced around his concrete prison and pushed himself to remember where and how he had been attacked. He remembered walking on the path through the woods beside Enid's house to where his truck was parked in the neighbor's yard. As Josh walked through the woods, he let his guard down briefly. When he heard movement to his left, he thought it was a small deer he had encountered several times. After all, it was broad daylight. By the time he realized he was wrong, it was too late. He felt a needle in his arm, through his shirt sleeve. After that, only darkness.

His head pounded. Whatever drugs this guy kept giving him produced an awful hangover. Since exercise and sweat are good for getting toxins out of the body, he did push-ups until his arms gave out and then jogged in place until his shins ached from pounding the concrete floor.

To keep his sanity, Josh meditated every day: when he first woke up and then before he fell asleep. This ritual not only gave him the mental endurance he needed to survive captivity but also helped him focus on what he remembered about this guy. Josh tried to retrieve every feature from his memory, even though he only had a flash of the guy before his world went black. Twice a day, his captor brought food, but he always wore a baseball cap pulled down low on his forehead. Otherwise, he didn't seem to care that Josh could see his face. That scared Josh.

During his meditations, Josh fought not to think about Enid. She would be worried sick by now and he was helpless to comfort her. Several times during his captivity, he questioned his ability to survive, a rare state of mind for him, so he focused on escaping. The little red light in the corner near the ceiling meant he was being watched 24/7, so when he meditated, he pretended to be asleep.

Did his captor know him? Was he someone Josh sent to prison? Or was Josh just a way of getting to Enid? That thought scared him more than anything. He knew a bit about stalkers and worked with several victims over the years. This guy was fixated on Enid, but what was the end game? Kill Josh and eliminate the competition? Then play on Enid's guilt until she became indebted to helping this creep? The questions were endless, and in Josh's foggy mental state, searching for answers was futile.

Wishing he had a piece of paper and pen to list what he remembered, Josh composed the only way he could—a mental list of all the bits and pieces. Every day, he went through the list, embedding it further into his memory.

So far, his mental list had these entries:

- Baseball cap covered most of the guy's hair – side burns and back were light brown
- Age mid thirties
- Height about 5'10"
- Slight Southern accent
- No limp or other obvious physical attributes
- A tattoo on left arm but mostly covered by long sleeves
- Eyes vivid blue—probably tinted contacts
- Strong physique
- Plastic surgery? His taut face had no wrinkles

- Perfect teeth - capped?

Either this guy was extremely vain about his appearance or he wanted to look much younger. Or perhaps he wanted to alter his looks. Nothing about this guy registered as being familiar.

Several times, Josh asked the guy what he wanted from him. There was never a reply, only a crooked smile that looked more like a smirk.

The cinder block enclosure where he was being held had no windows. The air was dank, and the floor was concrete. A basement? But there were no stairs. The guy came in from a door at the back of the room. Maybe this was a darkroom or storage room added onto another structure. Whatever it was, there was only one way in and out. In his partially drugged state, Josh wasn't sure he could overcome the guy, and if he failed, he might get himself killed.

Until he met Enid, he had not feared dying. During his undercover years working for the New Mexico State Police, he faced death many times and considered risk to be part of the job. Now he wanted to live, to have a life with Enid if she'd have him.

It was nearly time for the guy to come in and drop off a tray of food, and then he would return a little later to give Josh another shot, some kind of sedative. Josh would have to act fast. There was no room for error.

CHAPTER 47

Enid was sitting at the desk in her home office when she got notification of a message waiting for her on SecureDrop. She logged in and read a note from Talon:

"Are you ready to write about me yet? I'm going to give you an exclusive you can't turn down. Be at the Exxon station near the edge of Madden at 8:00 pm. Come alone. Remember, your man's life is in my hands."

Could she trust Agent Carlson not to jeopardize Josh's life if she shared this information with him? If Josh was still alive, she had no doubts Talon would kill him if something went wrong. After agonizing for several minutes, she called Carlson. "Don't make me regret this. I'm trying to do the right thing, but make no mistake, my priority is getting Josh back safely."

Carlson agreed to stay out of sight and to drive an F150, the vehicle of choice in these parts, complete with local high school bumper stickers. He would be at the gas station at one of the pumps, watching her.

Before they ended the call, Carlson said, "We've been checking your guy from college, that Cooper guy. Odd thing, he's fallen off the radar. No driver's license, no tax records. Just doesn't seem to exist any longer. We also checked for Talon, first and last name, just in case he was actually using his real name. Nothing. And we checked further on the Seth guy who worked at the distribution center.

Interestingly enough, he had a run-in with one of his girl-friends and she filed a restraining order against him. Seems he was stalking her. We've got him under surveillance, but I don't think he's our guy."

• • •

At precisely 8:00 pm, Enid parked beside the Exxon station. There was only one other car, and it was parked near the back of the building, so she assumed it belonged to the only employee inside. Within thirty seconds, a dark blue F150 pulled up to a gas pump and Carlson got out. Had she not known it was him, she wouldn't have recognized the man who was always meticulously dressed. Tonight, Carlson had on a baseball cap and appeared to be just any other guy in dad jeans.

The Exxon station was at the corner of the two-lane state highway leading into Madden and a county road leading to a rural, sparsely populated part of the county. She glanced at her iPhone. It was 8:05 pm. Maybe Talon was just testing her and had no intention of showing up. Carlson pretended to check his tires and pulled over to the nearby pump to add air.

And then headlights appeared on the highway coming into town. A dark van pulled up to the edge of the Exxon property and stopped. He was at least thirty feet away. The entire area was poorly lit, and Enid could not see anyone exiting the van. She lowered her window slightly, not far enough for anyone to reach inside. She glanced at Carlson who was back at the gas pump again. The employee inside could be getting suspicious of Carlson's odd behavior. But when she glanced inside the building, the young man at the counter was focused on the cell phone in his hand, seemingly oblivious to anything else going on.

The sound of the van door sliding caught her attention. And then within seconds, the van sped away, this time down the county road. Before she could process what happened, Carlson ran toward something lying on the ground. In the dark, she couldn't tell what shape or size the object was. Carlson was on his cell phone and then ran toward her car. He made a motion for her to lower the window. "Go home, I'll stop by later. Keep your doors locked. I'll call the sheriff's office to let them know what's going on."

"What do you mean? Is it . . .?"

"I've called in an APB for the van, although it was probably stolen."

"What was it he threw out?"

"I'm going to check it now. Stay here."

Disregarding Carlson's instructions, she ran toward the large bundle on the ground. It looked like a mummy wrapped in several layers of thick, dark plastic, probably painters' tarps. Three rows of silver duct tape encircled the bundle. "Please, tell me if it's Josh. I'm not leaving here until I know." She sounded hysterical, but right now, she didn't care.

"Then stand back. I don't need you to contaminate the area."

Carlson took several photos with his phone and then put on gloves and used a pocketknife to slice through the band of tape at one end. When he peeled back the plastic, a loud gasp filled the night air. "Get back further. This man is alive."

Instead, Enid moved toward the body. "It's not Josh. It's Ty, the reporter."

"Go home. I'll meet you there when I can. The deputy is just down the road. He'll follow you."

CHAPTER 48

After driving less than a mile from the Exxon station, the county deputy appeared behind her, flashing his headlights to signal his presence. But her own safety wasn't her biggest concern right now.

When they arrived at her house, the deputy walked her to the door and checked inside. When he announced, "all clear," she offered to make him a pot of coffee, which he accepted.

"I'll put it in a thermos and you can leave it on the porch when you're finished. Thanks for being here tonight."

"I'll just check the area first, so you'll see my flashlight around your yard."

Enid debated on trying to get some sleep while she waited for Carlson but knew it would be elusive tonight. She thought of Ty. He was alive, but for how long? Would he be able to give them information that would lead them to Josh?

These and other questions were swirling in her head when Carlson arrived several hours later. "Is Ty alive?" she asked as soon as he was inside.

"He's been beaten pretty badly. And he has a nasty head wound. Even if he lives, he may not remember anything."

"When will we know?"

"He's in surgery and being heavily guarded. I doubt we can question him anytime soon." He paused. "Look, I know this is torture for you, and I want to find Josh as much as you do. I assure you we're doing everything we can."

"Do you think he's holding Josh somewhere down that county road? Or was that just another diversion?"

"Your guess is as good as mine. We've got agents combing the area and we're tracing the plates, although they probably won't give us much information. This guy's not stupid." He pointed to the laptop on the dining table. "Can you contact him?"

"What do you want me to say to him other than to tell him he's a monster?"

Carlson looked at the coffee maker on the counter. "Mind if I get a cup of that?"

Enid got a cup from the cabinet. "I'll log into SecureDrop and see what he says."

"Tell him you've decided to write about him. See what happens."

Once she was on the system, she began typing, talking aloud so Carlson could hear her message to Talon: "Why did you hurt Ty?"

"Don't say that. He may think Ty is dead, and I don't want to tell him otherwise."

Enid deleted what she had written and started again: "Why Ty? What has he done to you? I'll write about you if you promise to release Josh unharmed."

"How long does it usually take him to respond?" Carlson asked."

"It depends."

Within a few minutes, she had a reply from Talon:

"He was trying to steal your fame. I did all of this for you not him. Besides, he's a hack reporter, nowhere near your level. I'm tired of waiting. Write an article about me and make it good. I want you to get credit."

She responded: "What about Josh. Will you release him?"

She waited for several minutes, but no reply came. She looked at Carlson. "I think Josh is already dead."

After only a few hours' sleep, Enid sat down to compose the hardest article she had ever written. Tears of exhaustion, fear, and frustration that she held back now poured out. When she could finally clean her face and get to work, she was determined to do it right. She owed it to Josh, no matter what.

Hours later, she had a first draft that was more of a chronological series of events than a cohesive story. At least she had documented everything she could remember. She printed the document and was reading it when a knock on her front door startled her. She heard a voice. "It's me. Agent Carlson. Can I come in?"

Even though she recognized the voice, Enid peeped out the front curtains to reassure herself. This was no time to take chances. When she opened the door, Carlson walked in. "I wanted to update you."

"Do you know something about Josh?" Her heart raced.

"Not yet. But Ty's head injury wasn't as severe as they first thought. He's out of surgery and the doctor says we can talk to him when he's awake."

While Enid appreciated Carlson's update, he hadn't told her anything to make her more optimistic about Josh's fate. "Thanks for letting me know."

"That's not all. We found the van."

Enid sat up straight. "Where?"

"It was abandoned about ten miles from nowhere down that old county road that runs beside the Exxon station. The crime scene techs are going through it now. If Talon left any evidence, they'll find it."

"He's too careful to leave any trace."

"At some point, even the craftiest ones get cocky and make a mistake. And when he does, we'll pounce on it."

"What about Ty's family?" Enid asked. "I don't know him well enough to know if there is someone who needs to be notified."

"We're checking that out. Apparently, he's from Chicago originally."

"That's odd. That's where Jack met Darren Smoak. You know, the guy—"

"I know who he is. In fact, we're bringing him in for questioning. There're too many coincidences in the case for my liking."

"Do you think Darren is involved in all this?"

"I'm not ruling anything out at this point. And if I learn anything about Josh, I promise I'll let you know immediately. Try not to worry."

Enid tilted her head slightly and gave him that look that Josh ribbed her about. "Yeah, right. I won't." She picked up the printout of the article. "You don't really want to print this, do you? I don't want to let him win."

"No, but he needs to think you're giving in to him."

• • •

At the hospital, Agent Carlson managed to convince the nurse to let him see Ty briefly. "I promise not to stay more than five minutes." Carlson tapped on the door before entering. "I'm Agent Whit Carlson of the State Law Enforcement Division. I'm coming in." Carlson pushed the door open. Ty was lying in bed, and his head was wrapped in gauze. A pale red splotch stained a portion of the bandage.

"I promised I'd be brief, so I need to get right to the point. What happened?"

Ty tried to talk but his mouth was so dry he couldn't form words. Carlson spotted a glass of water with a flexible straw in it on Ty's bedside table. "Here. Take a sip of water." Ty sipped a small amount and Carlson put the glass back on the table.

"What is your involvement with the man who calls himself Talon?"

Ty waited briefly before responding, his voice raspy. "He came to me about writing an article on Enid Blackwell at the *Tri-County Gazette*. This guy kept saying he loved her, well he actually said he 'revered her,' and he wanted to make her famous. He asked me to contact her and see if she'd work with me covering his story. He said it would propel her into the big time."

"Why did he choose you? Had you met him previously?"

"He says we met at a conference about the future of journalism. I don't remember him."

"So Talon is a journalist?"

Ty shrugged. "Everybody is a journalist these days, know what I mean? And like I said, I don't even remember meeting him. That was a huge conference, and I talked to a lot of people."

"Since I don't have much time right now, I'll skip to the end. Is Talon the person who attacked you?"

Ty nodded and then his face contorted in pain. "Aw,

man. My friggin' head is killing me."

"I won't be much longer. Why did he attack you?"

"I told him I was tired of playing games and told him to tell me his story, and I'd write it if Blackwell wouldn't."

"And?"

"And he went off the deep end, started screaming. I turned to leave and he hit me, and then I blacked out. Next thing I know, I'm here." He gestured around the hospital room with his arm. "Ungrateful son of a bitch."

"Do you know if he is holding Josh Hart captive?"

"Yeah, he wants to make a deal with Blackwell. If she'll go along with him, he'll release that Josh guy."

"But why is Talon doing all this?"

"I told you, man, he's friggin' infatuated with her. He's not right." Ty twirled his finger in a circle near his head. "Crazy."

"Is there anything you can tell me about where to find Talon or Josh?"

"I have no idea. We met at a place near Camden. An old warehouse."

The nurse stuck her head in the door. "You need to wrap it up."

"I will. Just give me one more minute," Carlson said.

With a stern look on her face, the nurse held up her forefinger to indicate the one-minute limit and shut the door.

"You work for a guy named Darren Smoak. He owns a few small newspapers, but I'm interested in his online newsletter on the dark web. Is Darren connected to Talon in any way you know of?"

"Talon told me that he met Darren in Chicago. Said he worked for him a little while."

"As a reporter?"

"Nah, I got the impression he did other things for him, if you know what I mean."

"And you have no idea who Talon is, other than what you've told me, and you don't know his real name?"

Ty shook his head. "Wait, I remember one time he answered his phone, and he said something like 'Coop here.'"

"Coop? As in chicken coop?"

The nurse opened the door. "That's it. Your time is up. My patient needs his rest."

Carlson put his business card on the bedside table. "We've got someone stationed outside, so this guy Talon can't get to you. Call me if you remember anything, no matter how small."

Walking down the hospital corridor, Carlson called his office. "I'm going down to USC School of Journalism. I'll be in later."

CHAPTER 50

The University of South Carolina is a downtown campus located in the heart of Columbia, the capital city. Parking spaces are scarce. The School of Journalism and Mass Communication is housed in an old brick building on campus. Carlson rode around the area several times before finding a spot where he could safely park, although it was a no-parking zone. He put his SLED placard on the dashboard, hoping the campus police would see it before writing him a ticket.

Once inside the building, a lanky student, dressed more like a street bum than the students Carlson remembered from his college days, directed Carlson to the information office.

"May I help you?" the woman asked.

"Thanks, Colleen," Carlson said glancing at her name tag. He assumed since there was no last name, she wouldn't be offended, but you can never tell these days. "I need to talk to someone about a former student." He showed her his SLED identification.

She studied the ID and smiled. "Well, that would be me. How can I help you?"

Carlson flipped through his notebook and gave her the name of Marcus Alton Cooper, as well as a copy of the article written by Enid and Marcus more than a decade ago.

"That's an old edition of our student newsletter, the *Daily*

Gamecock."

"Yes, I know, and I'm trying to find out anything about this Cooper guy that I can. We can keep this informal if you'd like, or I can come back with a warrant."

Colleen appeared to force a smile. "That won't be necessary unless you need something I can't give you. What do you want to know specifically?"

"I need to track this guy down, so anything you can give me would help."

"The admissions office can give you specifics on Cooper's enrollment." She paused, probably debating how much she wanted to offer voluntarily. "But if you want more specific information, Professor Kirkley was teaching here then, and he might be able to help you. If you'd like, I'll see if he can meet with you."

"Terrific. Thanks, Colleen."

• • •

Fifteen minutes later, Carlson was sitting across the desk from a grandfatherly looking guy whose bushy eyebrows and thick white mustache made him look like Wilfred Brimley's twin. Whereas the twinkle in his eyes reminded Carlson of St. Nick. "Thanks for taking the time to talk with me."

"Sure thing, young man." Kirkley said. "Mind if I ask why you want to find this fella Cooper?"

"Just to ask him some questions about an ongoing investigation. He may know something that can help us."

Kirkley studied the article Carlson gave him. "I'd like to tell you I remember all my students." He laughed. "But I don't. Some days I can't remember what I had for breakfast. Or even if I remembered to eat. But I digress." He looked at the article again. "I remember Ms. Morgan. She had a lot of promise. She and that guy she married, they both went on to work for the Associated Press."

"Her name is Blackwell now. Enid Morgan married Cade Blackwell, who was also in the same journalism class."

"Yes, I remember Cade. A bit arrogant, but talented." Kirkley walked over to a cabinet brimming with papers. After a few minutes, he pulled out a file. "Ah, here it is." He sat down at his desk again and thumbed through a stack of papers. "I try to keep up with all my students, which is impossible. But this guy Cooper, he wrote an essay on fame that so intrigued me I've kept a copy all these years."

"Can I see that?" Carlson asked.

"Sure, I'll make you a copy." He called out to a student assistant who promptly made a copy at a nearby copy machine.

Carlson skimmed the essay. "I don't have a literary bone in me, so you'll have to tell me what's so great about this article."

"I wouldn't say it was great. That would be too generous. But it was intriguing, and I like people who think differently." He poked at the article with his finger. "This guy was so fixated on fame that it was a bit disturbing. But it was also well-written. The guy had potential, no doubt about it."

"What happened to him? Do you know?"

"He flunked out because he didn't do the work. He had the talent, but he didn't have the determination to see it through. When he left school, he told me he was going to be famous one day, and that I should remember his name. Considering his lackadaisical attitude about assignments, I found that amusing." Kirkley scratched his head. "But what do I know?"

"Have you heard from him since he left?"

"No, not from him. But one of his classmates told me Cooper had lost a ton of weight and had all that excess skin surgically removed. This friend said Cooper is unrecognizable now. You see, he was a big guy. Big around the middle, I mean." Kirkley laughed. "Anyway, his friend told me Cooper had gone to Los Angeles." He held up his hand. "No, wait. That's not right. Chicago. That's where it was. Cooper went to work for a gossip rag. You know, one of those papers that writes about who's dating who, who's eating where, that sort of thing. Then I heard later Cooper left town because he was so reviled."

Carlson realized he was holding his breath. "Do you know where he is now?"

Kirkley scratched his stomach and stared at the ceiling. "Someone told me something about him not too long ago, but, hell, I can't remember what. If I think of it, I'll let you know."

"Thanks, I'd appreciate it. It's important. Before I go, one last question. Did Cooper cause any problems in class? I understand he was infatuated with Ms. Blackwell, that is Miss Morgan."

Kirkley threw his head back and laughed. "Hell yeah it caused problems. I thought Cooper and Blackwell would come to blows when Cooper kept sniffing around Morgan. The only reason they didn't, I think, is because Cooper was so fat and unattractive that Blackwell didn't feel threatened, just annoyed."

"Do you remember how Miss Morgan reacted to Cooper's advances?"

"Not really. She was a kind-hearted person and mostly saw the good in people. Mind you now, she could hold her own with any of them. Great debater and a talented writer. But she didn't look for trouble, so I doubt she caused Cooper any problems herself."

Carlson stood up and handed his card to Kirkley. "If you think of anything else, let me know. I really appreciate your time."

"Good luck, young man."

When Carlson got back to his car, he didn't see a parking ticket and was glad not to have to deal with the campus police.

As he navigated through downtown Columbia traffic, his mind was on fame—not his own, but Cooper's. Was his essay merely a class assignment? Or was it a glimpse into the mind of a madman?

CHAPTER 51

Josh feigned sleep once again while planning his escape. Something had changed about his captor, but Josh couldn't pinpoint what it was. In some ways, his captor seemed more comfortable around Josh. Sometimes he even chatted with Josh, like he was an old friend and they were sitting in a bar together. Hopefully, that meant the man would drop his guard long enough for Josh to make a move.

But the man also appeared to be more focused and determined now. Had he decided what to do with Josh? Kill him? Use him to bargain with Enid? That thought scared him because she would probably do almost anything to set Josh free. He tried not to think about the worst-case scenarios.

Nighttime would be the best for his escape. But since there were no windows, he couldn't tell what time of day it was. The dim ceiling light was always on. Sometimes it was much cooler, so he assumed it was after sundown. He would wait for the temperature to drop.

And then what? He couldn't break out. The only door was steel with a deadbolt. He would have to overcome his captor. The man was strong enough to handle Josh after he was drugged. And when the man brought meals, Josh could see muscles beneath his shirt, whereas Josh felt himself getting weaker from confinement and a limited diet. Since Josh had been in captivity, he had eaten mostly brown rice and bananas with an occasional apple, and a small amount water with each meal. Enid would probably approve of his diet, but it wasn't enough to keep up his strength. Josh would have to rely on the element of surprise.

But what was outside of this concrete block structure? Were they in a town? In a rural area? What would Josh face even if he got out? He'd worry about that part when it happened. Right now, he just had to escape.

As Josh did his daily hundred push-ups, his mind was playing a movie of how he would overcome the man. He simply could not fail. There was too much at stake for him and for Enid. By the time Josh finished his exercises, he was mentally prepared to do what had to be done. He prayed he was also physically ready.

When his captor delivered the evening meal, Josh was ready to execute his plan. One thing Josh knew was that this man would be able to tell if Josh behaved differently. When the door opened and the man came inside and locked the door behind him, Josh pretended to be resting. Through half-shut eyes, Josh watched the man put the keys in his left pocket. He must be left-handed. Josh mentally added that detail to his list.

"Ready to eat?" the man asked.

Josh sat up and pretended to be groggy from sleep. "Uh. Yeah. Sure." Josh rubbed his eyes with his hands. "Is it filet mignon or lobster tonight? Or perhaps escargot? Not that I really want to eat snails. Unless you've got a good French champagne to go with it. Actually, I'd prefer a Spanish cava, if you have it."

The man laughed and kneeled down to put the tray on the floor in front of Josh. "Bon appetit." Before the man could straighten up, Josh lunged forward and grabbed the man's legs below the knees, pulling them forward and forcing his captor to fall backwards. "Son of bitch," the man said. "You'll pay for this."

As Josh jumped onto his captor and pinned him to the floor, he gave silent thanks to his high school wrestling coach who had been relentless in making Josh practice long hours. Then Josh's undercover training took over. He hit the left side of the man's neck with the edge of his hand, striking the carotid artery. The man appeared to be out cold, but for added security, Josh switched hands and struck the right carotid also.

Josh reached into the man's left pocket and grabbed the keys. He had to act quickly. Steadying his breathing the way he had trained himself through meditation, Josh put the keys in the door and opened it. Before he stopped to assess his surroundings, Josh locked the door behind him and pulled on the handle to make sure it wouldn't open.

Now that he was free, where was he? It was nearly dark. As Josh's eyes adjusted, he looked around. Nothing else was in sight. No buildings or houses. Just open fields. There had to be a car somewhere, but where? Josh ran to the other side of the building. Leaning against the cinder block wall was a mountain bike. *Are you kidding me?* Laughing out loud, Josh jumped on the bike and headed across the field. As Josh tried to think of his next move, he wished he had searched his captor for a cell phone,. For now, he would just keep pedaling.

CHAPTER 52

Ty looked uncomfortable, probably from the pain but likely also from the fact that Agent Carlson sat beside his hospital bed. "Do I need an attorney?" Ty asked.

"You're not under arrest. Is there some reason you think you're in trouble?"

Ty closed his eyes and laid his head back against the pillow. "Can we get this over with? My head is throbbing."

"I won't keep you long, and if we need to do this later, we can. But as I'm sure you understand, time is of the essence."

Ty partially opened his eyes. "Go ahead."

"What is your relationship with the man who captured you, the man known as Talon?"

"None really, or at least not until recently. He contacted me with an offer to give me an exclusive to the kidnapping of Winifred Tucker, that young girl."

"Did you notify the authorities?"

Ty remained silent.

"I didn't think so. And you agreed to work with him?"

"Yes, but he made it clear he wanted Enid Blackwell to get the credit. So I contacted her, but she wanted nothing to do with it."

"So how did you end up like garbage dumped on the street?"

"Talon and I met, and he was upset, said he needed to let

her know he was serious. He thought I should be able to convince her to work with me on the articles. He kept saying he was helping her, and she just didn't realize it. I commented that I couldn't force her to do anything. He got upset, and when I turned to leave the meeting, he hit me with something. That's the last thing I remember until I woke up here."

"Can you describe him for me? What was his physical appearance?"

"He's mid-thirties, I'd guess. He's less than six feet tall, I'd say more like 5'10", well built—obviously works out." Ty paused and closed his eyes. "His hair was dyed. I saw where his roots had grown out. His natural hair was lighter. And his teeth were capped. Nobody has perfect teeth like that."

"Did he have an accent or say anything about where he's from?"

"He's a Southerner. Tried to disguise his accent but every now and then, he slipped up when he got agitated. There are certain words Southerners just can't seem to say without giving themselves away."

"Did he tell you anything about how he knew Ms. Blackwell?"

"He said he admired her since he first met her. Actually, he said he worshipped her. Kinda creepy, if you ask me." Ty pointed to a pitcher of water on the bedside table. "Can you give me some water? My throat is killing me."

Carlson poured Ty a glass of water. He took several long sips. "Thanks, man."

"Did he mention where he first met Ms. Blackwell?"

"Not that I recall. To be honest, I was getting tired of his shtick, so I didn't pay much attention. I wanted to know what was in it for me. Know what I mean?"

Carlson smiled slightly and nodded. "You work for the *Nosy Rag*. Tell me why you went there from a reputable paper like the *State*."

Ty broke eye contact with Carlson and looked away toward the wall opposite his bed. "Stupid. That's all I can say. I really bought that line about how we would become the most influential alternative newspaper in the region. It was all bullshit."

Carlson smiled. "I would have thought with a name like the *Nosy Rag*, you would have guessed it wasn't too reputable."

Ty looked back at Carlson. "You'd think, right? But journalism is dying, at least in the traditional sense. People say they want objective reporting, but what they really want to know is the dirt. They want reporters to get nosy and get answers. Know what I mean?"

"Who recruited you to leave the *State* and go to the *Nosy Rag*?"

"Darren."

"Would that be Darren Smoak?"

Ty nodded.

"Did he tell you he was trying to buy the paper where Ms. Blackwell was working at the time?"

"I found out later."

"Do you think there was any connection between Talon and Smoak?"

"You mean like golfing buddies?"

Carlson shrugged. "That or some other way."

"Not really. Darren pushed me to stay on top of the Talon story. He said it was my only priority."

Carlson leaned forward and rested his elbows on his

thighs. "Didn't you question all this business with Talon and Smoak? Didn't it seem odd to you?"

Ty raised his hands slightly. "Man, I'm just trying to make a living. I'm not paid to figure out these things."

Carlson looked at his notes but before he could resume his questioning, the nurse came in. "That's enough for now," she said. "He needs to rest."

Ty looked relieved and laid his head back against the pillow.

"I'll catch you later. If you think of anything, write it down and get in touch with me. You've got my card. Okay?"

Eyes shut, Ty replied, "Sure thing, man. Sure thing."

CHAPTER 53

Josh stopped pedaling after what seemed about fifteen minutes. Based on his cycling experience from years ago, he estimated he had been moving at least seven miles an hour. At one time, he was an accomplished rider. Now, given the years away from the sport and the effects of captivity, he was breathing heavily. The bike's fat tires were good for stability on dirt trails but took more effort.

He slowed slightly and glanced over his shoulder. It was fully dark now and there were no streetlights, houses, or structures nearby. He could easily get hurt with no clear vision of where he was going, so Josh decided to find cover and wait. After getting off the bike and catching his breath, he looked around for a place to spend the night.

His captor must know the area well and likely knew a way out of the building where Josh had been held. He might even have a spare key in his other pocket. But as much as Josh wanted to keep moving, he had no idea where he was going. There were no sounds of cars on a highway, no trains. Nothing. The total darkness and lack of sound reminded him of his stay on the island of Bonaire in the Caribbean. He stayed with a friend who lived in an old research cabin on the nature preserve. At night, you could hold your hand in front of your face and not see it because of a total absence of light. And the only sounds were the wild donkeys braying.

Just ahead of him on the trail, there was a large tree with

what looked like a hollow in its trunk. Josh got off the bike and stuck his hand in the opening, hoping nothing reached back at him. The opening appeared large enough for him to squeeze into. He glanced around and saw a thicket of bushes with branches that bent over and touched the ground. A perfect place to hide the bike.

By the time he stashed the bike and settled into the hollow of the tree, he was exhausted. The escape, the bike ride, and fear had all taken a toll on him mentally and physically. Even though he was tired, he would have trouble sleeping. But he had to try.

The sounds of the night were comforting. Josh grew up in New Mexico and spent many nights sleeping under the stars both as a child and an adult. When he worked undercover as a drug dealer for the New Mexico State Police, the gang he hung out with slept anywhere they could, which was often outdoors in the desert. An owl overhead pulled him back to the present.

Though he tried to relax, a million questions swirled in his mind. Was Enid safe? Who was his captor? How would he find help? Josh leaned his head back and tried to focus on the 4-7-8 breathing technique he often used to fall asleep. He inhaled through his nose for four seconds, held his breath for seven seconds, and then exhaled through pursed lips for eight seconds. After repeating this process several times, Josh dozed off.

• • •

Enid tossed and turned, tried to sleep but couldn't turn off her mind. Something was different. She could feel it. But what? Sleep just wasn't possible tonight.

Her heart ached when she admitted to herself that Josh was likely dead. Talon had no reason to keep him alive. And if Josh tried to escape, which he surely would, Talon would kill him if possible. Tears rolled down her face and into her ears. What would her life be like without Josh? Where would she go? What would she do? She could always stay in Madden and work for Jack, but she could never feel the same way again about being a reporter. Being too visible was dangerous these days.

She had never thought about her own death, but tonight no topic was off limits. Dying didn't scare her, but being old and alone terrified her. Anytime these thoughts had come up in the past, she told herself the ideal place to exist was somewhere between not wanting to live forever but not wanting to die either. That's where she was now—that in-between place. If Josh was dead, she would go on living. Maybe she would find someone else eventually, or maybe she would stay single. She was strong, a survivor.

Whatever Josh's fate, she would honor the vow she had made to him. She would do her best to live a happy productive life. After tossing and turning for what seemed like an eternity, she eventually fell asleep.

CHAPTER 54

Something made a noise that woke Enid. What was it? After a few seconds, she realized her cell phone was vibrating on her nightstand. She reached over and grabbed it. "Hello."

"Enid, this is Cade. Are you okay?"

She glanced at the time. "It's 4:45 am. Where are you?"

Cade laughed. "In London. You know, where I live. Look, I realize it's early there, but I've got a bunch of meetings starting in a few minutes and I wanted to call you while I could."

"This must be important for you to call this early."

"I know where Cooper is."

Enid sat up in bed. "What? Are you serious? But how?"

"You asked me to check the Associated Press' list of reporters. Olivia found Marcus Alton Cooper's name on a list of previous employees, from about ten years ago."

"How does that help us?"

"Hold on. I'm getting to that. Later, he came back to work for the AP, not as an employee but as a stringer doing odd stories here and there."

"That's something mostly newbies do. Why would he do that?"

"Olivia has a friend who told her, confidentially of course, that Marcus got into some trouble in Chicago working for another paper. The only way AP would let him come back was as a contractor, not an employee."

"You said you also know where he is now."

"He's in South Carolina, or at least he was at the time. It's a rural route address. She couldn't find anything recent on him. I'll text you his last known address. But only if you promise not to go there. Let the authorities handle it."

When the text came through, she saw that the address was in Fairfield County, not far away. How long had he been stalking her? She exhaled deeply to release the tension.

"No word on Josh yet?" Cade asked.

"No, nothing. Look, I appreciate your getting this information for me. Thank Olivia for me. I'm sure the FBI either already knows this or will find it soon, but if they ask, I won't tell them how I got it." She glanced at the time again. "If your meeting starts in a few minutes, you'd better get going."

"Yeah, you're right. Oh, before I go, just wanted to let you know the wedding has been postponed."

"Until when?"

"Indefinitely. I'll tell you more later." He paused. "Please don't look for this guy yourself. I couldn't live with myself if something happened to you."

"I'll be careful. But I am going to find Josh."

A brief silence. "I hope you do. And I mean that. You deserve a great guy like him. Keep me posted. Gotta go."

A few hours later, after a shower and quick breakfast, she texted Jack and Ginger to tell them she would be unavailable for the day. They would wonder what was going on, but she didn't want to involve them, at least not yet. Now she had to figure out how to shed the county deputy assigned to watch her. She looked through the few things Josh had left at her house and found the extra set of truck keys he made in case she needed them.

Before putting her plan into action, she wrote a note and

left it on her refrigerator door, held by a "Madden Matters" magnet the town had issued last year to celebrate its growth. Dressed in a baseball cap, jeans, and boots, she slipped out the back door and ran for the woods toward her neighbor's house.

Seeing Josh's truck flooded her with emotions, which she pushed back. No time for sentimentality now. She cranked the engine and checked the gas gauge, which showed a full tank. Josh always told her to keep her car gassed because "you never know what might happen." Right now, she was grateful for his survivalist mentality. She checked her cell phone to be sure she had Agent Carlson's and the deputy's number in her favorites list, in case she needed to make a quick call.

If there was ever a time to pray, it was now. *Please, God. Let me find Josh.* She adjusted the rearview mirror and backed the pickup onto the county road.

• • •

When Enid arrived at the Ridgeway Post Office, she texted the deputy assigned to her. She didn't want to get him in trouble or to have him worry needlessly. He could have her call triangulated by SLED or the FBI, but she would be long gone before they traced her general location. Besides, she wasn't a suspect. Her brief text stated simply that she had personal business to attend to and that she was safe. After the text, she turned her phone off. She also had the burner phone with her that Jack had given her in case she needed to make calls.

The lady at the post office counter was eager to help when Enid showed her the rural route address. "Can you give me a map of the area this route covers?"

"We don't have that information to hand out, but there's a website online where you can get a map. It's a commercial site for a data company that certifies postal addresses." She scribbled on a piece of paper and handed it to Enid. "That should give you what you need."

"Thanks. I tried to use Google maps but that didn't work."

The woman smiled. "No, not with rural routes."

"I appreciate this information. Just one more question. Does this route cover mostly residential areas?"

The postal clerk looked at the route number again. "Mostly residential. I think around three hundred houses and just a handful of businesses. A good bit of open land too. Good luck with your search. And you be careful. Those are good people, but some won't appreciate strangers snooping around, so you be careful." She paused. "You looking for someone in particular?"

Enid debated on how honest she should be. "Actually, I am. We were old college pals. His name is Marcus Alton Cooper."

"Cooper. That's a good Scottish name. I dated a Cooper guy once, but I don't think I know your fella."

"Thanks again for your help."

Enid returned to her car and pulled up the website, inputting the rural route number. As the clerk said, it was mostly residential. She headed down the two-lane highway, and before long, she was in a rural part of the county.

She knew from research she had done for a series of articles that farming had not been a significant segment of Fairfield County's economy for many years, but the area was dotted with small boutique farms specializing in meats and vegetables. During the summer, the farmer's market offered everything from watermelons to microgreens. Now the county's economy relied on heavy equipment and other manufacturing companies that moved into the area. Ample land, relatively low taxes, and an available workforce made the county attractive to these companies.

As she drove down the main road on the rural route, none of the box numbers were close to the one she was looking for. Frustrated, she glanced at her watch. She had been driving for nearly an hour before she pulled off to the side of the road. Had she really thought she would just drive up to a house on this rural road, knock on the door, and announce she was there to rescue Josh? The absurdity of her quest made her laugh aloud at her own stupidity. But she had to do something. SLED and the FBI were working around the clock, but somehow Talon still managed to elude them. They would get him eventually, but it might be too late for Josh. She turned on her phone and texted the deputy to tell him she was headed home.

CHAPTER 55

Agent Carlson was furious after getting a call from the Bowman County Sheriff's office that Enid slipped away from her house without the deputy's knowledge. And he was worried. They traced the Cooper guy, whom the investigation team now called Talon, to a neighboring county. Enid Blackwell may have found the same information through her sources. Suspecting that Cooper had journalism roots, Carlson's team learned he worked for the Associated Press a couple of years ago. They had not been able to find a current address, but perhaps Blackwell had more information than they did. Journalists were not bound by the same bureaucratic constraints as law enforcement and often had incredibly good sources for information. Cade Blackwell worked for the London office of the AP and likely helped her. Of course, she could have just gotten cabin fever and needed to get out, away from the deputy's watchful eye. But knowing her reputation for investigating on her own, Carlson worried.

Today he was interviewing Darren Smoak. Carlson tried to maintain a neutral attitude toward anyone he interviewed, but he already didn't like Darren Smoak. All the information gathered on him pointed to a despicable guy. And since Carlson was already in a bad mood about Enid's little road trip, the day wasn't starting off well.

Carlson walked down the hall to the room where Smoak

214 · RAEGAN TELLER

was waiting. "Hello, Mr. Smoak. I'm Agent Whit Carlson with the South Carolina Law Enforcement Division. We appreciate you coming in to talk with us."

"My attorney wasn't too happy I came in voluntarily, so let's keep this short and to the point."

"I understand your concern, but you're not under arrest, nor are you a suspect at this time. We asked you to come in because your name keeps coming up in our investigation of a missing person."

"I thought the Tucker girl returned home safely."

"You are correct. She did. But her kidnapper is at large, and another person has gone missing. We thought you might be able to shed some light on some of these connections to you that surfaced."

"How can I help you when I don't know who's missing?"

"Do you know Joshua Hart?"

"Not personally, no. I've heard of him. He used to be sheriff, right?"

"Yes, he was sheriff of Bowman County and before that he was the police chief of Madden."

"So what's this got to do with me? Has something happened to him?" Smoak held up his hand. "Oh, wait. I think one of the reporters at the *Tri-County Gazette* is dating him." He shrugged. "Still, what's that got to do with me?"

"Let's talk about one of your employees, Ty Browning."

Smoak's eyes narrowed. "What about him?"

"Are you aware he was kidnapped and is now under medical care?"

"I know he hasn't checked in for almost a week. But he's a contractor, not an employee, so he doesn't have to check in daily."

Carlson studied Smoak's face. In the nearly twenty years

he had worked for SLED, he had interviewed hundreds of people. Some were good liars, some were bad. Most of the time, Carlson could tell. But as much as Carlson wanted Smoak to be a despicable liar, he seemed to be telling the truth, at least about the questions he had answered. "It appears you own a couple of small-town newspapers, is that correct?"

"Yes."

"And your intention was to buy the *Tri-County Gazette*. Is that correct?"

"I checked it out, but it turned out to be a bad investment."

"I see. And you also own, or partially own, an online, underground newspaper called the *Nosy Rag*. Is that correct?" For the first time during the interview, Carlson noticed a change in Smoak's demeanor.

Smoak shifted his weight in the chair and fiddled with his watchband. "Yes, I own part of it."

"A third, is that correct?"

"That's about right."

"And Ty works for that newspaper, which I believe is only accessible on the dark web." Carlson locked eyes with Smoak. "Why is that?"

Smoak shifted in his chair again. "Look, I'm trying to be cooperative here, but where is this going?"

Ignoring his question, Carlson continued. "Were you aware that your employee, Ty Browning, has been in contact on more than one occasion with a man known as Talon, whom we believe kidnapped Winifred Tucker, may have killed a reporter, and then abducted Ty Browning? This Talon guy may have also taken Joshua Hart, who is now a missing person."

Smoak put both hands on the edge of the table and pushed his chair back slightly. "Whoa. I had no idea Ty was involved with this Talon guy. He came to me for a job after the *State* newspaper wouldn't let him do articles on the kidnapping, at least not the way Ty wanted to write them. We run a pretty loose operation at the *Nosy Rag*. And to be honest, our readers don't subscribe for the news articles. But we try to give our reporters some leeway to do what they want."

"Instead of news, you mean it's mostly illegal gun sales, prostitution, and sometimes even a little human trafficking." Carlson leaned forward. "Is that about right?"

Smoak threw up his hands in a surrender motion. "Okay, that's it. If you can tie the paper to anything specific, go for it. And if you have any more questions, you can contact my attorney. But for the record, I'm not involved in any way with whatever arrangement Ty set up with Talon. I only provide working capital for the underground paper in exchange for a decent return on my investment. The other two owners, the ones who established the paper, are the decision makers. But I know they are not directly involved in trafficking, kidnapping, or anything like that. We provide a service to people who want to buy and sell, let's say, unique things." Smoak stood up. "If you want me to have my attorney call you, I will."

"Not yet. Just don't leave town without checking in."

"Actually, I'm leaving this afternoon to return to Chicago. I came here to buy the local paper, but since that deal is off, I have no reason to hang around this sleepy little place."

"I understand. Then let us know where you can be reached if needed. Just out of curiosity, why would you want to buy small-town newspapers? You come from a wealthy family and you don't seem like the kind of guy who wants to edit news about the local farmer's market and craft shows."

Smoak laughed. "You know, there's a decent market out there for well-run, small-town papers. Compared to the big papers that are struggling to stay afloat, some of the small ones do pretty good. I keep getting reminded that some people still want local news." He shrugged. "I don't get it, but that's the way it is. You can't get rich running a small paper, but now and then I run across retired newspaper guys like Jack Johnson who jump at the chance to own their own paper. For some, it's a vanity thing, but for others, the news is in their blood. I worked in it for a while but never got attached. Now I just buy 'em up, the small papers, and resell them to the highest bidder. For a small profit to cover my expenses, you understand."

"And I'm sure your services are appreciated. Like I said, give us your forwarding address. We'll be in touch if we need anything further." As Smoak was leaving, Carlson added, "By the way, you ever run across a reporter named Marcus Alton Cooper?"

A broad smile covered Smoak's face. "Coop? Yeah, I know him. We met at a friend's pool party and he asked me for a job. I got him an entry level position at my father's investment firm. He didn't stay long though. He wasn't cut out for the business and went back into the news world. Oddly enough, he sends me Christmas and birthday cards every year. Weird the way he just keeps hanging on to me. We were never like great buds or anything. Why do you ask?"

"Just curious. His name came up somewhere. Would you happen to have his address?"

Smoak tapped a few times on his iPhone and then turned the screen to where Carlson could see it. "I save addresses and contact information on almost everybody. Occupational habit. Here, this is the last one I have for him. I think that's somewhere around this area, isn't it?"

"Next county." Carlson tried not to show his excitement. "Mind if I write that down?"

"Sure, no problem."

Carlson wrote the address on his notepad. "Well, thanks again for coming in."

CHAPTER 56

Several times during the night, Josh managed to sleep lightly, but every little noise woke him. After his confinement, it felt good to be outside, but he had to rest and prepare himself physically and mentally for what lay ahead. He felt something crawling on his neck and slapped it away.

By the time daylight arrived, Josh was wide awake and making plans. He peeped outside the tree hollow, scanning the area. When he stepped out to stretch, his back and legs were stiff and sore. He did a few jumping jacks to limber up. He walked over to the bush where he hid the bike, pulled it out, and brushed off the dirt.

Last night, it was difficult to see anything or to get his bearings. In daylight, it wasn't much better. As much as he wanted to remain out of sight, he had to stay on the dirt path because going through the dense woods would be slow and even more dangerous. He had to find help. His biggest fear right now was that he was going to pedal right up to his captor's house. As far as he could tell, the path he was on now was the only way to and from the structure where he had been held, although he didn't look to see if the path also went in the other direction from the shed.

Optimistic by nature, Josh told himself he had a fifty percent chance his captor lived in the opposite direction. But he was also a realist and would stay alert and ready to hide if needed.

Josh kneeled to look at the dirt path. He was relieved to see there were no obvious mountain bike tracks. However, the path was covered with pine needles and leaves, so it was hard to tell. After examining the bicycle tires for any cuts, he rode off toward an unknown destination.

With some sleep and slightly less anxiety than yesterday, pedaling was easier than it had been the previous night. He looked up and scanned the area above the trees. Were those power lines in the distance? He pulled off the path and walked until the cables were directly overhead. At least he was in civilization. And what was that sound? He listened closely. Nothing. But then he heard it again. It was definitely a large truck on a road.

Once Josh left the path, it was impossible to ride the bike in the dense brush, so he pushed it along as he jogged toward the sound. A short distance later, a two-lane paved road appeared. Looking in both directions, he saw no vehicles. And then he looked overhead to find the eastern path of the sun. It didn't help much since he had no idea where he was, but it made him feel better to get his bearings.

While he was relieved to find the road, he was more exposed now and had to be careful. Josh moved back to stand behind a large bush where he could hear oncoming vehicles but still be mostly out of sight.

After what seemed like a long time, he was ready to abandon his plan and begin pedaling down the road. Instead, he cautioned himself to be patient and continued waiting.

Eventually, he heard something coming. It sounded more like a car. Should he flag the person down? Surely his captor had found a way out of the building by now. What if it was him? In hand-to-hand combat, Josh could take down almost anyone. But unarmed, he couldn't fight a knife, outrun a bullet, or peddle as fast as a car.

When a vehicle came around the slight curve into sight, Josh exhaled loudly to release the tension. It appeared to be a farm truck, an old pickup with rust on the hood. But that was no guarantee of safety since Josh had no idea what the man drove.

Josh took a deep breath, stepped toward the road, and held up his hand. The truck passed by slowly enough for Josh to see it was an elderly woman. He stepped back from the road and prepared to wait for another car. And then he saw the one brake light on the truck as it pulled off to the side of the road. When she started backing up, he jogged toward her.

The passenger window was partially down, and Josh kept his distance so as not to alarm the woman. "Hello, ma'am. I'm a bit lost and wondered if I might ride back here in the back of your truck to wherever you're going. I just need to get to a phone."

The woman stared at him a bit before responding. "You lost and you ain't got no phone?"

Josh smiled and tried to look harmless. "It's a long story, and I understand you being nervous about picking up a stranger. That's why I can sit back here." She continued staring and didn't respond. "Please, ma'am. I just need to get to a phone."

"Alright then, git on in the back. I'm headed to the IGA store up the road. Need sugar for my canning."

"Thank you, ma'am." He put his foot on the tire to hoist himself onto the back of the pickup.

"That your bike back there?"

"Yes, but I'll get it later."

"It'll sprout legs and walk away by the time you git back

222 · RAEGAN TELLER

here, but it's up to you. Throw it on the back if you want to."

"That's nice of you. I think I will take it along. Might need it." Josh jogged back to where his bike leaned against a tree. He glanced back at the truck, afraid she might take off without him.

Within a few minutes, he and the bike were headed down the highway with the old lady. He wished he had money to pay her, but his captor had taken everything from him.

About thirty minutes later, they pulled into a large grocery store in a strip mall. A dozen or so cars were in the parking lot. He jumped out of the truck and lowered the tailgate to get the bike.

The woman walked around to the back of the truck. She was no more than five feet tall, with short silver hair, wearing tan khaki pants and a flannel shirt. "There ain't no pay phones here. How you gonna call somebody?"

"I'm hoping maybe the store will let me use theirs."

She made a guttural sound. "Not likely. Nothing free these days." She waved at an elderly man getting out of his car. "Hey, Horace, come here a second."

The man hobbled over to the pickup truck, favoring his left leg. "What you need?" The man eyed Josh from head to toe.

"Let this young man borrow your phone."

The man surveyed Josh again. "Well, I don't know about that."

"Good grief, old man. Just give him your phone. He ain't gonna run off with it."

The man reached in his pocket and pulled out a flip phone. "It ain't fancy, but it works fine for what I need. Make it quick though. I only get a certain amount of minutes a month, and my son gets upset when I go over."

"Yes, sir. I will. Thank you." Josh had everyone he called regularly in his favorites, so he had not actually had to remember Enid's number in a long time. The first number he dialed was incorrect. He looked at the man and woman who were both staring at him. "Sorry, I'm trying to remember the number. Let me try again." He said a silent prayer he'd get it right this time. He did, but he got Enid's voice mail. He didn't want to alarm the woman, so he tried to act casual as he left a message. "Hi, Enid. It's me, Josh. I'm at the IGA Store . . ." He paused and looked at the woman. "Ma'am, can you please tell me where we are?"

"We're in Winnsboro. You must not be from around here."

"No ma'am." He returned to the message. "I'm at the IGA grocery store in Winnsboro. Can you please come get me? Thanks . . . And I love you." Josh flipped the phone shut and handed it to the man. "Thanks very much. I'd like to repay you, but I don't have any money with me. If you want to give me your address, I'll mail you some money later."

Horace waved his hand and walked back toward his car. "Nah, don't worry 'bout it."

"We don't want your money, son," the woman said. "Just go have a good life. See 'ya," she said as she walked toward the store entrance.

CHAPTER 57

Enid was busy vacuuming her home office when the call came through. Since her phone was on the kitchen counter, she didn't hear it ringing. It was nearly twenty minutes later when she saw the message.

At first, she was sure it was another cruel joke. But after playing it over and over, the voice was definitely Josh's. She tapped on the number. It rang several times but no answer. She tried again. This time, a man answered.

"Hello, sir. I got a call from a friend from this number. His name is Josh. Is he there?"

"You must mean that young man at the IGA. Borrowed my phone. He was still up at the store when I left."

"Is there more than one IGA store in Winnsboro?"

The man laughed. "No, just the one. Not far from here. Want me to go find him for you?"

"No, but thank you for helping him." She wanted to ask if Josh was okay but didn't want to involve this man any further.

"Sure thing."

Enid searched on her phone for the IGA's address and grabbed her tote. Was this another one of Talon's jokes? But the message definitely sounded like Josh. When she ran outside toward her car, the deputy got out and came over to her. "You okay?"

"Yes. Follow me but stay back." When the deputy looked

puzzled, she yelled. "Please, just do as I ask."

The deputy got back in his car. When Enid pulled onto the highway, he drove behind her but kept his distance.

The store was at least a forty-five-minute drive from her house. Could it really be Josh? She refused to get her hopes up again since she had been duped twice before, and she wasn't sure she could take much more of Talon's games.

• • •

When Enid saw the big red and white IGA sign, she said a silent prayer. *Please let it be Josh. Please, God. And let him be okay.* She pulled into the parking lot but saw no one standing near the store's entrance or in the parking lot. In the rearview mirror, she saw the deputy pull in from the highway and park at the far end of the lot.

Should she stop and get out? After all that had happened recently, she no longer trusted her instincts. She tried to think. What would Josh do? If he was in danger, he would hide someplace where he could see her coming but not be seen. But what if he was hurt? Surely he would have said so in his message or the man whose phone he borrowed would have mentioned it. What if Josh thought she wasn't coming? The questions kept racing through her head.

She glanced toward the deputy's car. He was on his radio, likely notifying others that something was going on, so she had to act fast before the place was flooded with SLED agents and county police. After surveying the parking lot again, she drove slowly toward the right side of the store and then around to the back side loading area. A slight hill covered in kudzu and small pine trees was behind the store. She stopped driving and waited. And then, some kind of movement on the hill caught her attention. A man on a bicycle was coming toward her. Was it Talon? Has this all been an elaborate trap? And in broad daylight?

She made sure the car doors were locked as she continued to watch the bicyclist. When he got closer, she could tell it was Josh, wearing that great big smile she loved so much. Her mind flooded with flashbacks. Josh holding her, smiling. Josh cooking his family chili recipe for her, smiling as he stood at the stove. Only now could she admit to herself she thought she'd never see that smile again.

She jumped out of the car and threw herself at him. "Josh. Oh, Josh." No words came to mind that seemed adequate for the joy and overwhelming relief.

"Oh, baby. I love you." Josh glanced around. "Come on, let's get out of here." He ran around to the passenger side. "Wait, I need to take this bike. It might have fingerprints."

She popped the trunk of her car and they managed to get it mostly in. "We don't have any way to keep the trunk lid down." She paused. "Wait, the deputy is over there. We'll get him to take it in. His trunk is much bigger than mine." She called the deputy on her phone and asked him to come over to her car.

When he arrived, she instructed Josh. "You stay in the car. I'll take care of this."

The deputy looked at both of them. "Is that Josh Hart?"

Enid felt her face might split open from the wide grin on her face. "Yes, it is. But you need to take this bike in as evidence. There may be fingerprints. I'll call agent Carlson and see where he wants to meet us."

While the deputy put on gloves and secured the bike, Enid called Carlson to give him the news. "Yes, it's him this time and he appears to be fine."

"I am fine. Just hungry and tired," Josh said.

"Alright," Enid said to Carlson. "We'll meet you at my house. Josh says to run prints on the bike the deputy is bringing in." After the call, she leaned over and kissed Josh. "I thought I'd never see you again."

CHAPTER 58

By the time Enid and Josh got to her house, Carlson was already there, and another SLED car was parked in the yard. Carlson followed them into the house.

"Mind if we meet at the kitchen table?" Enid asked. "I thought I'd make Josh a sandwich."

"Sounds good. I'd love a cup of coffee if you have one." He turned to Josh. "Do you need medical attention?"

"No, I'm fine. Nothing a meal, a shower, and some sleep won't solve."

Enid made sandwiches and coffee for Carlson and Josh. "Do you want me to stay, or would you prefer to talk to Josh alone?"

"You can stay. You'll be bombarded soon when word gets to the FBI and the local press that Josh is safe, so this might be my only opportunity to talk to you." He asked Josh, "Do you know who abducted you?"

"No. I've had a lot of time to think about it. I've never seen him before, I'm sure."

"Did he say anything that might be a clue to his identity?"

"He talked very little. When he did, his comments were smug. It was as though he had something personal against me, but he never gave me a clue as to what it was."

"If it was Talon, he's probably jealous of your relationship with Enid," Carlson said. "How did you get away?"

"My instincts told me to wait until he got comfortable

around me before I made a move. He's fairly strong. When I felt it was time, I managed to catch him off guard." For the next hour, between bites of two sandwiches and several cups of coffee, Josh went through his escape ordeal and what he could remember of his captor's description from the list in his head. He turned to Enid. "That woman who dropped me off at the IGA, she probably saved my life."

Enid put her hand on Josh's and squeezed it tightly. "I want to thank her when we can, as well as the man who loaned you his phone."

"I'll need that phone number Josh called from," Carlson said to Enid. "We can find the man and the woman with it."

Enid gave him the number from her phone.

"Do you have any idea where this cinder block building is where you were held?" Carlson asked Josh.

Josh shook his head. "No idea at all. And for all I know, he may still be locked up in it. But he seemed like the kind of guy who would have a contingency plan."

"Let's back up then. When you were picked up on the highway, which direction did she drive toward?"

"Southwest. We drove for about ten minutes on some road that wasn't marked and then onto Highway 34 for about twenty minutes."

Carlson smiled. "I wish all my victims were as reliable as you are." He flipped his notebook shut. "I'll see if they've processed that bike for prints."

"Mind if I go to the boy's room? It's been a while."

"Of course, go ahead," Carlson said. "And if you want to try to grab a few winks, now would be the time to do it. You're going to be busy for a while answering more questions."

When Josh left the room, Carlson said to Enid, "You put

yourself, Josh, and the deputy in harm's way. Why didn't you call me?"

"Are we really going to do this now? Can't it wait?"

"And when were you planning on telling me about Marcus Alton Cooper?"

"I knew that if I found him, you had already done so, but likely wouldn't tell me."

"That's a lot of assumptions you made." Josh returned, and Carlson pointed his finger at her. "We'll talk later. For now, let's just be thankful for a happy ending."

"It's not over until you put that guy behind bars," Josh said.

Carlson's phone rang and he went outside on the porch to take the call. When he came in, he said to Josh, "A county deputy is on the way to pick you up. He'll drop you back off here later." Carlson looked at Enid. "In the meantime, don't go sneaking off again. We'll keep a man outside until this Talon guy is captured."

CHAPTER 59

When Josh returned to Enid's house, it was nearly midnight. His smile had faded and his shoulders were slightly stooped. "You look frightful," she said.

"Thanks. I feel frightful. Let's just say the sheriff and FBI were thorough. I need to sleep. Do you mind?"

"Of course not. You go ahead, and I'll be in soon."

"You need to rest too. They'll interview you in the morning."

"I can't wait," Enid said, smiling.

"Let's not forget they're the good guys."

"I know, and I'm grateful for all they're doing. You go on and get some sleep."

Enid opened her laptop and began making notes. It was easy to forget details and she wanted to capture everything she could remember. When she glanced at the time again, more than an hour had passed. She turned off the computer and took off her shoes as she entered the bedroom. Josh was sound asleep, so she didn't turn on the light to find her sleep shirt. Instead, she just slipped off her clothes and crawled into bed.

As much as she wanted to talk to Josh and hold him, she also wanted him to rest. Her mind was racing as she laid next to him, but eventually, she fell asleep from exhaustion.

When her phone vibrated on the nightstand, she looked at the time—4:00 am. It was her old phone, her original phone number, so it could be anyone. She grabbed the phone and went into the hallway, shutting the bedroom door behind her. "Hello," she said as softly as she could. "Who is this?"

"Do you want to thank me now?"

Enid's chest tightened at the familiar altered voice. "Why should I thank you, you bastard?"

"Now, now. I spared your man, I returned Miss Tucker. I think you owe me."

"And you killed a friend of mine. You need to turn yourself in. I know who you are, Marcus. That's right; I know you're Marcus Alton Cooper. That was clever the way you made an anagram out of your middle name. As I recall, you were smart in school and had a promising career in journalism. All the professors said so. What happened to you?"

"I'm impressed with your investigative skills and surprised you even remembered me. After all, I was madly in love with you at the time, but you only had eyes for that self-centered, pompous Cade Blackwell."

"Why did you do all of this, Marcus? Was it just to get my attention?"

"I wanted you to experience loss and disappointment, just as I did."

"Well, you accomplished that. Not just for me, but think of what you've done to Mia's family. Why did you have to kill her? You could have let her go too."

"She had promise, too much in fact, and would become your competition. I didn't want her to steal your thunder. Besides, she was an arrogant bitch."

"Turn yourself in. You need help, and they'll see that you get it."

Marcus laughed. "Always the optimist, just like in school.

Trying to find the humanity in the vilest of situations." He sighed. "Oh well. I actually will turn myself in, but on one condition."

"I can't make deals with you. You need to talk to the authorities, but I'll tell them you want to come in."

"Don't bother. I'll let them know. They've got a tracer on your phone, so I need to go. But I'll discuss my conditions with them. I'll leave a message on SecureDrop." Before Enid could reply, the call ended.

Within fifteen minutes, a message notification appeared: "My dear Enid, our time together is coming to an end. Remember, I have loved you far longer than Cade has, or that superhero you're with now. As I told you earlier, I will turn myself in, but only if the authorities agree to my terms. I want you to interview me and to publish our story. That's the only statement I will make. I promised to make you famous, and I always keep my promises. I want to be interviewed at your house, as your guest. Tell me when to be there. Oh, and yes, I fully expect SLED and the FBI to be there also. Don't worry. I won't hurt you and will give myself up freely after the interview. Your devoted admirer, Talon."

CHAPTER 60

Enid shook Josh awake. "Sorry to wake you up, but I need to talk to you. Right now."

Josh opened his eyes and glanced around the room. "Are you alright?"

"I'm fine, but we need to talk. Come on, I'll make you some coffee."

Enid waited until Josh had consumed his first cup before telling him about the call and message from Marcus. "That's crazy. You can't do it," Josh said.

"But what harm will it do if he agrees to come in and is arrested? He needs help."

"Please don't tell me you feel sorry for this guy."

"It's not that. I won't forget the pain and suffering he caused so many people because of his obsession with me. But that's also what makes me feel responsible. I know he'll eventually be caught anyway, but I owe it to Mia's parents to make sure he's brought to justice as quickly as possible. Can't you understand that?"

Josh leaned over and kissed her. "Of course. That's one of the many things I love about you. You're smart, compassionate, and totally sexy."

Enid pulled away. "Please don't joke. This is serious."

"You're right, but I was serious. Let's call Whit Carlson now. I'll shower and get dressed. Appears we're having house guests soon."

• • •

SLED agent Whit Carlson was at Enid's house in less than an hour. "I agree with Josh. This is crazy. We found the building where he was held captive. It was on a rural piece of property Cooper rented. When we interviewed the owner, he said Cooper told him he accidentally locked himself inside the storage buildings and asked the owner to come get him out. Cooper gave his name as Marcus Morgan when he rented the property."

"He used my maiden name," Enid said. "That's creepy."

"The crime lab is gathering prints, DNA and other forensic evidence from the building, and the property owner is cooperating. We'll nab Cooper soon, so you don't have to go along with this crazy scheme of his to have you interview him."

"But he knows he has nothing to lose by withholding his statement if we say no. This may be the only opportunity to get critical details that will help put him behind bars forever."

Josh took her hand and said to Carlson, "She wants to do it. Let's set it up."

After a brief conversation about the logistics of the interview, Enid, Josh, and Carlson agreed to Talon's terms. Carlson called his FBI counterpart and the Bowman County sheriff, who agreed to let SLED make the arrest since they were the leads in this case. SLED and the sheriff agreed to let Enid do the interview, which would be recorded by a SLED agent posing as a newspaper reporter. But the interview would be used as evidence, not for a newspaper article as Cooper requested. In return for the interview with Enid,

Cooper agreed to surrender without incident. It was scheduled for that afternoon, which allowed Enid and the
authorities time to develop questions that sounded convinc-
ing enough to be a reporter's questions but sound enough
to give the authorities what they needed for conviction.

CHAPTER 61

As the time for the interview got closer, Enid's chest was tight and her stomach churning. "I think I'm going to be sick," she said to Carlson. Josh agreed to stay out of sight but remain within earshot.

"You'll be fine," Carlson said to Enid. He pointed to the camera man. "By the way, this is Agent Phillip Liu. We call him Phil. He's also an experienced videographer."

"Hi, Phil. Thanks for doing this for us," Enid said.

"No problem." He pointed to the *Tri-County Gazette* logo on his borrowed tee shirt. "And thank you for the shirt."

"We made those for a charity event last year. Glad I saved one."

Carlson looked at Enid. "You ready to roll?"

Enid nodded.

Carlson stood and walked to the front door. "I'll wait out here for Cooper."

Enid took deep breaths to calm her nerves. "I'm fine," she called out to Josh in the next room. "This is surreal, you know. I can't believe after all that's happened, Marcus is going to drive up and sit down with me like it's a normal interview."

"I admit it's pretty unusual," Josh called from the back room.

Enid heard a vehicle on the gravel driveway and went to the front window. A man, mid-thirties, got out and straightened his trousers before walking toward Agent Carlson, standing on the front porch. She assumed the man was another SLED or FBI agent. And then she heard Carlson's voice. "Marcus Alton Cooper?"

The man smiled and nodded. "Of course."

Enid's hand flew to her mouth as she gasped. Even though she knew Marcus lost weight and transformed himself after college, she wasn't prepared for this total change. Unlike the dumpy, nerdy guy from journalism school, this man was attractive and meticulously dressed.

"I need to check you for weapons," she heard Carlson say.

"Sure, no problem."

Seconds later, the door opened and there stood the man who had been stalking her relentlessly, who had kidnapped Winifred, killed Mia, and abducted Ty and Josh. She quickly took a sip from the nearby water bottle to ease her nerves.

"Hello, Enid my love," Cooper said when he walked into her living room. "Good to see you again. You're as beautiful as ever."

Her mind flooded with images, questions, and revulsion. How could she have a normal conversation with this man? And then she reminded herself why she agreed to it—to put this guy away. "What should I call you in the article?" she asked him.

"I rather like Talon, don't you? You yourself said it was a clever anagram. And I need to appear as inhuman as possible to make this interview grab your readers." He smiled. "Don't you agree, Miss Morgan?"

Talon knew her name was Blackwell, so she refused to take the bait. "Alright then, let's proceed."

Carlson interrupted and spoke to Cooper. "Before you

start, I need to advise you of your rights, as you are under arrest. You have the right to remain silent. Anything you say can and will be used against you in a court of law. You have the right to an attorney. If you cannot afford an attorney, one will be provided for you. Do you understand these rights as I've explained them to you?"

"Sure thing," Cooper said smiling.

Carlson continued. "I want to make sure you understand this interview is a de facto statement and confession of guilt you are voluntarily giving without representation. Do you understand what I am saying?"

"Oh, sure," Cooper said, still smiling.

"Do you have any questions before Ms. Blackwell proceeds?"

Talon smiled as he locked his gaze on Enid. "No, I understand fully." He then turned to Carlson. "And do you agree that this interview can be made public for the article? You do understand that I'm doing this for Enid."

Carlson crossed his arms on his chest. "As we discussed earlier, we cannot and will not make all the details public. But, upon approval of the content, Ms. Blackwell will be allowed to publish an edited version as an exclusive article, per our agreement."

"And you understand, I will not make any further statements to the police?"

"Yes," Carlson said.

"Good. Then let's get started," Talon said.

"I'll begin with the obvious question first, which is why did you abduct three people, killing one of them?" Enid asked.

"As you know, Miss Morgan, we were in journalism classes together at the University of South Carolina. In fact, we even shared a byline for an article on . . ." He paused and appeared to be thinking. "Ah, yes, it was on whether a journalism degree was a good investment."

"Yes, I recall that article," Enid said. "Please answer the question."

"Of course, the answer to that question we posed, by the way, is no, at least for you and me. I was punished for writing the truth, and you . . ." He swept his arm around the room. "You've ended up here in . . . Where are we exactly?"

"We're just outside of Madden, South Carolina."

"Ah, yes, the lovely, small town of Madden that's about to become a bigger town of idiots working at the distribution center. But that's another story. Where was I? Oh, yes. Well you see, I wanted you to have a second chance at fame. No one thinks a small-town newspaper reporter can cover meaty stories. But you've already done some very good pieces about cold case murders, human trafficking, and elder abuse." He clapped his hands silently. "Very impressive, Miss Morgan."

"For the record, as you know, my name is Enid Blackwell. Morgan was my maiden name when you knew me."

Talon smiled. "Yes, of course. So sorry for the confusion. I still think of you as sweet Miss Morgan."

"Can you please answer my original question, which is why did you abduct three people, killing one of them?"

Cooper shifted in his chair and crossed his legs, interlocking his fingers and resting his hands on his knee. "Of course, you want a motive. As I've said several times, I wanted to make you famous, to build your brand as a journalist. You deserve nothing but the best. My life is over, but you have an opportunity to go big now," he said, dramatically waving his arms through the air. "I lost track of you for a while, but when your articles came out in the Associated Press, I started keeping an eye on you again." He sighed. "Ah, yes, I killed that reporter. I believe you said her name was Mia? Anyway, she was sure to cause you problems later, and instead of accepting my power over her, she tried to attack me. She became a nuisance, the way she was snooping around trying to cover your story about Winifred Tucker's abduction. I kidnapped Miss Tucker after I read the article on her scholarship. You see, I just borrowed her for a while to give you an opportunity to write the story. I didn't appreciate that reporter, Mia, taking it from you." He turned to Carlson. "Yes, Miss Tucker and the reporter were just victims of circumstance and opportunity. Sad, but true."

Cooper then turned back to Enid. "But Josh Hart, well, I admit that was planned. After you wouldn't play nice with me, I had to get your attention." He smiled. "And it worked. Now you know what it felt like when I lost you to Cade Blackwell."

Enid glanced at Agent Carlson. As if he knew she was going to explode, he shook his head slightly, signaling her not to take Cooper's baiting.

She took a deep breath and continued. "What is your relationship with reporter Ty Browning, a reporter with the *Nosy Rag* and formerly with the *State* newspaper?"

Cooper uncrossed his legs and sat back in his seat, shrugging. "Met him at a reporter's conference. He seemed hungry to, let's say, elevate his status, so I used him. Foolishly, I thought you'd jump at the chance to work with Ty on my story. But when you didn't, I had to alter my plans a bit." He laughed. "You're unpredictable. I like that."

"And what is your relationship with Darren Smoak, one of the owners of the *Nosy Rag*?"

Cooper posed in an imitation of The Thinker, the famous sculpture by Auguste Rodin. He stayed in that position briefly and then sat up again. "I knew him briefly. His father gave me a crap job at his investment firm, but I didn't stay long. They didn't appreciate what I had to offer."

For the next two hours, Enid asked questions prepared by the FBI, SLED, and the county sheriff's office, trying to make it appear as a routine interview. Cooper was not an idiot and surely realized what was going on, but he continued gazing affectionately at Enid, laughing at inappropriate times, and looking smug all the while.

Finally, Cooper slapped his hands on his thighs and said, "Okay. We're done here." He smiled at Enid. "You've got what you need for a great story, and I can't wait to read it." He looked at Carlson. "That's the agreement, remember? I get to read her story."

"Sure," Carlson said.

Cooper stood up and put his hands behind his back to be handcuffed. "Well, that was fun. And I'll say no more about this matter. Ever."

CHAPTER 62

After Cooper was taken away, Josh joined Carlson and Enid in her living room. "I don't know how you kept your composure," Josh said. "I wanted to run out and strangle the guy."

Enid held her hands out in front to show they were shaking. "I'm a wreck, as you can see. And I'll never publish that monster's story."

"You did a great job. Of course, I'd have preferred to interrogate him myself, but since he's refused to give a statement, we'll work with what we've got. It's enough to convict him," Carlson said.

Agent Liu, who was packing up his video equipment, patted the camera and added. "I agree. we've got his confession and enough details to put him away for life. All in front of witnesses, I might add. Nice job, Ms. Blackwell. If you ever want to come to work for SLED, I'm sure we can arrange an interview."

"Thanks, but I'm ready for a normal life again. Will he get the death penalty for killing Mia?"

Carlson shook his head. "No, I'm afraid not. Part of the agreement was that he would tell us everything in exchange for taking the death penalty off the table. Mia's parents agreed. In fact, they are adamantly against the death penalty for anyone. They just want him put away for life. And while I agree with you that we don't want to make this guy famous with your article, we did agree for you to publish an edited version. And trust me, it will meet the terms of our agreement, but it won't be the story Cooper hoped for."

"But he wanted to make Enid famous," Josh said. "And I'm afraid he'll get that, even with an edited article. The other papers will focus as much on Enid as on Cooper." He looked at her. "You'll have offers for big positions coming from all over the country."

Enid put her arm through Josh's. "We'll talk about that later."

Josh then asked Carlson. "What about Seth, the guy from the diner I talked to? Did you ever find him?"

"He was creepy, I agree," Enid said. "I wondered about him also."

"We found him," Carlson said. "He owed years of child support, so he skipped town when he heard we were looking for him. Turned out to be just another deadbeat dad. There are more of them out there than you want to know. And we'll be talking to Darren Smoak also, or at least the FBI will, to follow up on the allegations that he's using the classified sections of his newspapers for illegal purposes across state and national lines."

"Why would he bother with small papers when he's also publishing on the dark web paper?" Josh asked.

"I have no idea. These allegations may turn out to be nothing, but the FBI will find out what he's up to." Carlson walked to the front door and turned back to Enid. "I know this has been a terrible experience for you. For what it's worth, I think you handled it well. Not everyone could have kept their wits about them the way you did. Your interview will put Cooper away for the rest of his life."

"Thanks. I'd like to think this could never happen again,

but I know it can. It's a dangerous world."

"Well, try to go on with your life and put this behind you." He looked at Josh. "Good luck to you too. We'll have to get together over a couple of beers and catch up soon."

Josh put his arm around Enid and squeezed her shoulders. "Sounds good. I'm ready for normal too."

CHAPTER 63

In less than twenty-four hours, the tightly edited version of Talon's interview went public. It was published by all the major newspapers in the state, as well as in a special edition of the *Tri-County Gazette*. As Talon and Josh predicted, Enid got offers from several large newspapers. In that respect, Talon got what he wanted.

After being overwhelmed with interview requests, Enid stopped answering her old phone number, but when the burner phone rang, she recognized Jack's number.

"You feel up to a meeting later today?" he asked.

"Sure. I doubt I'll get anything else done anyway. I'll be in after lunch. That work?"

After Enid agreed on a time with Jack, Enid asked Josh if they could sit on the porch and talk. She made him a pot of coffee and made herself a cup of tea. "I don't have anything other than a protein bar to offer you with your coffee."

Josh laughed. "Thanks, but I'll pass. I've got to teach you to cook."

"Or you can just cook for me. Come on, let's sit outside. I want to experience normal again."

They sat side by side in silence on the porch in the wicker settee for nearly ten minutes before Josh spoke. "I can't imagine what you must have gone through. I'll never understand why, if that Talon guy loved you so much, he wanted to make you miserable."

"Stalkers have a complicated relationship with their targets. I did research for an article last year and learned quite a lot. Rejection often sets them in motion."

"But it was more than a decade ago when you met him."

"I assume his obsession with me went dormant until something else in his life triggered the memories. When he found me again, that decade meant nothing to him. It was like we were in class together again, except this time, his appearance was transformed and he was more confident he could attract me." Enid took Josh's hand and squeezed it. "In addition to being narcissistic, stalkers are also possessive and live in a fantasy world. I'm thankful he didn't kill you, but I'm sick about Mia's death. I feel responsible."

"You didn't hurt Mia and you didn't put her in harm's way. It's sad and unfortunate, but not your fault."

"Why do you think he didn't kill you?"

"He seemed to be conflicted about me. I could feel it. He wanted to hate me but something else was going on too. I guess we'll never know. He promised never to speak again about what happened, and I believe him. He'd make an interesting book." He smiled. "And I know a great writer who could pull it off."

"Oh, no. There's no way I'd spend a year writing about that creep. I just want to forget him."

"I'm kidding. I wouldn't want you anywhere near him again."

Enid took a sip of tea. "You know, all this has made me reassess my life. You know, what I want, what I don't want."

"Don't let that monster dictate your life or make you alter your plans. You probably need to wait a while before you make any major decisions. In the meantime, you know Jack will take you back in a heartbeat."

248 · RAEGAN TELLER

"I know you're right. I just need to enjoy life for a bit before I force myself into any big plans about the future. But I still want to leave the paper. I might write an occasional article for Jack, but I need to step back and see if being a reporter is really what I want. It's a changing industry, and I'm not sure I want to be a part of it." She leaned her head on Josh's shoulder. "What about you? You still going to get your PI license?"

Josh laughed. "You crushed me when you said I was a cliche." He turned and buried his face in her hair, kissing her head. "But at least you made me think about my decision. While I was held captive, I did some reassessing too."

Enid sat up and turned to look at him. "And? What did you decide?"

"I like putting bad guys away and making the world a bit safer. I know that sounds corny, and I realize that when I put one away, three more take their place. But I do what I can."

"Does that mean you're going back into law enforcement?"

He scrunched his face. "Would you be upset if I said yes?" He held up his hand. "Before you say anything I want to say something else."

Enid smiled. "Okay, say something else. I'm listening."

"Whatever I do, I want you to be with me. If you hate the idea of me being a cop, then I'll drive a forklift at the distribution center. Or I'll—"

"Stop it. You are a cop. That's who you are, and I would never discourage you from being true to yourself. You deserve to be happy."

Josh took both of her hands in his. "Enid Blackwell, I want you to be happy with me. Will you marry me?"

Enid's mouth opened but she couldn't talk. "I . . . Whoa, that was sudden."

"Not really. I've had a lot of solitary time to think about us. I made up my mind when I was in New Mexico that I would ask you when I returned. I love you, Enid Blackwell, and I want you to be my wife. Forever."

"Before I answer you, where would we go if you went back into law enforcement? Do you want to go back to New Mexico?"

"I promise you I will not go back into undercover work. That's too much time away from you, and it changes a person. When I was held captive in that building, I kept thinking about when I was police chief in Madden. I didn't appreciate it at the time, but I really loved that work, getting to know the town folks. And I really miss the ladies in town making me pies and cookies." He grinned. "Since you won't bake for me."

She lightly punched his arm with her fist. "Very funny. But Pete's in that job and doing great. You wouldn't try to take it away from him, would you?"

"Goodness no. Besides, he fixes the mayor's computer when she needs it, so I know if she had to choose between us, she'd keep Pete. I guess we'll have to find another small town to call home, that is if that's okay with you. But if you'd prefer a bigger city, we'll go wherever you want to live to pursue your career."

"Right now, I don't know what my career will be. And you know what? I'm really okay with that. For now, at least. But I have one more question. Are you going to ask me to have a bunch of kids?"

Josh threw back his head and laughed. "God, no. We might get a dog though, or even a cat, or both, if that's okay with you. And I do need to teach you to cook, just for survival."

Enid leaned in and kissed Josh. "Well, then I guess it's official. We're engaged!"

CHAPTER 64

When Enid went into the newspaper office to meet with Jack, the parking lot was filled with vehicles from various news and television crews. They had a right to make a living and she wanted to support them, but right now she just couldn't bring herself to stop and answer questions. "Later, guys. I promise," she called out to them as she went inside.

"Wow," Ginger said. "You're quite the celebrity. Thanks for gracing us with your presence."

"Stop it. You know I hate this kind of attention. Where's Jack? In his office?"

"Yes, ma'am. Waiting for you."

When Enid walked into Jack's office, he was reared back in his chair with his eyes closed. Despite his insistence that his cancer had not returned and that he felt good, he just didn't look like the same old Jack. But then, this ordeal had been tough on everyone.

"Hey, Jack. Is this still a good time?" Enid asked.

He sat up in his chair. "Of course. Always a good time to talk with you. Have a seat."

She sat in one of the chairs across from his desk. "Paper ready to go?"

"I just sent it to print." He paused. "What do you think about Darren's plan to go all-digital?"

"Before I answer that, does this mean you're keeping the paper?"

252 · RAEGAN TELLER

"Well, I'm certainly not selling it to Darren. However, he did put me in touch with a woman who is interested. She sounded sincere when I talked with her, but since she knows Darren, I'll have my attorney check her out real close. She says she only knows him through a mutual friend."

"So you've already talked with her?"

"Yes, and as a matter of fact, she's coming here tomorrow. I've made arrangements for her to stay at the Glitter Lake Inn. We're having dinner there tomorrow night. From the short conversations we've had, it appears we have a lot in common. She's a former senior editor, and her husband died of cancer." Jack tapped a few letters on the keyboard and turned his monitor around so Enid could see the screen. "That's her."

Enid studied the smiling woman's image. She had shoulder length, brunette hair, and an athletic build. "She's very pretty."

"Yes, she's attractive. I'll send you her bio. I'd love your thoughts about her."

"Of course." She paused. "But I want to be clear about my intentions regarding my work with the paper. I don't want to mislead you."

"I know you're leaving. Well, I don't actually know, but you've been restless for a while, long before this Talon guy began stalking you. And with Josh back in town, I figured you two would . . ." Jack sighed. "Whatever you do, you know I'll support you. And Josh. I love you both like family. But I have to admit the thought of you leaving breaks my heart."

"We've done some good work together, haven't we? I'll never forget what you've done for me. In a way, I feel like I'm letting you down, since you've mentored me for bigger and better things."

"Bigger and better isn't always the answer. I learned that the hard way. You're smarter than I am so you learned that lesson quicker. There are so many times I've wished I could go back and spend more time with my wife. I had no idea she would be taken from me so early in our lives." He slapped the table with his palms and smiled. "But you. Look at the great work you've done here. I'm so proud of you. Whatever you decide to do, I know you'll do it well."

"I thought I knew what my future would be. Eventually, I planned to go on to a bigger newspaper. But then I learned to love Madden and its small-town ways. The truth is, though, life is changing here, and I don't know what this place will be like in another five to ten years. As they say, you can't stop progress. As for me, I've come to realize I want someone to share my life with. At one time, I thought that person was Cade, but we were just too different in the ways that matter. We'll always be friends."

"You really love Josh, don't you?"

Enid nodded. "I didn't know just how much until I thought I'd lost him. He's kind, sensitive, and quite romantic." She blushed slightly. "But what I love most is his determination to do what's right. As he said, he is a lawman. I know I'll worry about him a lot, but I want him to do what makes him happy."

"Don't overlook making yourself happy. Too many women spend their lives sacrificing for their families and put their own needs on hold."

"I won't. But I need some time to figure out what I want to do. Journalism is changing so much. Maybe I'll learn to embrace it, but for now I want to learn to cook." She laughed. "Josh has promised to teach me. Maybe I'll even

do some writing along the way. It's nice for a change not to
have a plan. I'm just going to live in the moment, perhaps
for the first time in my life, and to find my own truth. I'll
figure it out when the time is right." She paused. "Anyway,
I'm not going to walk out until you find my replacement. I
won't leave you shorthanded."

"You know how you keep saying Ginger would make a
great reporter? Well, we're going to find out. I've got her
scheduled to do a couple of articles to get her feet wet. As
you know, she's a great investigator, so it's possible she'll
take up your mantle. Not right away, of course. She needs
experience."

"That's wonderful. I'll be glad to help train her. Although, she'll mostly be investigating stolen chickens and
vandalized storage sheds."

Jack smiled. "That's about right. And thanks, I was
counting on your helping to develop her." He slapped his
palm to his forehead. "Oh, I forgot to tell you why I asked
you to come by. I wanted to tell you in person."

"What's that?"

"I've decided to adopt Rachel. I know she's an adult now,
but South Carolina allows you to adopt another adult. I want
to make sure she's taken care of. And she needs family as
much as I do. She's graduating as a cyber forensics investigator this year, and I want to give adoption papers to her as
a gift."

"That's wonderful. I know she will be overjoyed. She
loves you so much."

"And I love her." Jack wiped his eyes. "Now let's not get
too sappy here. I have a paper to run, at least for a while
longer."

"I love you, Jack Johnson. We must promise to stay

close, no matter what."

"I love you too. Yes, we'll absolutely stay in touch."

On the way out of the office, Enid stopped by to congratulate Ginger and to offer whatever support and training she needed.

Uncharacteristically, Ginger gave Enid a hug. "I hoped you would agree to train me. I want to learn from the best."

"Well, I don't know about that, but I have learned a thing or two I'm happy to pass along. Let's sit down tomorrow and work on a plan."

When Enid walked outside, the reporters were still camped out waiting for her. She forced herself to smile. When they rushed toward her, she held up her hands in surrender. "Alright, I'll keep my promise. After all, reporters need to support each other."

For the next thirty minutes, she stood in the parking lot answering their questions. She gave them what she could, being careful not to divulge anything outside of her agreements with the authorities. "Just one more question, and then I've got to go." Enid pointed to a young woman near the back of the group who had her hand up. "You there, in the back. What is your question?"

"Why did you become a reporter?"

The question surprised Enid since it was seemingly unrelated to the Talon case. When she and Cade were first married, they talked endlessly about their idealistic career goals in journalism, one of the few things they had in common. Both agreed on what was most important to them as reporters, so it was easy for Enid to respond to the young woman's question. "To learn the truth."

∞

PLEASE . . .
A humble request from the author

Thank you for taking time from your busy schedule to read this (or any other) book. The world needs more readers like you.

I hope you enjoyed *Time to Prey*. If so, please do me a big favor and leave a review on Amazon and/or Goodreads. Reviews encourage other readers to explore authors with whom they may not be familiar.

Thank you in advance for your review!

www.Amazon.com

www.Goodreads.com

AUTHOR NOTES

I met Enid Blackwell when I began writing *Murder in Madden* in 2013. We didn't get along at first. After all, we're both hardheaded redheads. I quickly learned she had her own ideas about her life and how the stories would be written. After resisting her intrusion for nearly two years, I relented and finished *Murder in Madden* in 2016, told the way Enid wanted it.

Over the course of the next four books, Enid and I became best friends—the kind of friend you can tell anything to, who won't judge you, who cares deeply about your welfare and wants you to be happy above all else. Someone recently told me Enid and I are more alike than I'll admit.

Having learned early on that good fiction requires conflict, tension, suspense, and emotional upheaval, I've put my dear friend Enid through a lot of turmoil in these five volumes. When I began writing *Time to Prey*, I warned her this story would be her darkest hour yet. But I also reminded her of the words of Thomas Fuller, an English theologian and historian, who uttered these now famous words in 1650: "It's always darkest before the dawn."

Like all the books in the Enid Blackwell series, this one was also inspired by an actual event. When I was looking for an idea for this fifth book, my husband, a wonderful storyteller, suggested I look to Larry Gene Bell for inspiration. If you lived in South Carolina in 1985, you will likely remember his name. He kidnapped and killed two young women, ages 17 and 9. We lived not too far from his first victim, Shari Smith. What I remember most is how he taunted Smith's family. Thirty-six years later, I still recall the horror of those cases.

Once I decided to use the Bell case as my inspiration, I warned Enid to buckle up, because it was going to be a rough ride for both of us. I also asked her to trust me to do the right thing.

As anticipated, writing *Time to Prey* was difficult for me. I began in June 2020 during the Covid-19 pandemic. My mother-in-law had just died of the virus, and like many others, I had trouble focusing on anything. I also questioned the purpose of writing a fictional murder mystery when so many people, including several of my friends, were dying in real life. But I reminded myself I write for entertainment. It's odd, but true, that fictional murder can be entertaining to those of us who enjoy solving puzzles and finding the bad guy. And fiction is a wonderful escape, so I pushed myself to get going. But I didn't have my usual drive, and it was a slow, sometimes painful process. I also learned that my beloved editor, Ramona DeFelice Long, was dying of cancer and wouldn't be able to finish the series with me. Sadly, she died in October 2020.

Reliving the Larry Gene Bell case was also disturbing. I had nightmares a few times as I recalled those awful murders and his taunting. But when I wanted to quit, Enid threw Fuller's words back at me and reminded me of the promise I made to her.

Many of my readers have asked if this will be the final book in the series. It may be. I never intended to write a series, and when I finally committed to do so, I declared there would be four books. And yet, here we are with book number five, so who knows what will happen next. I will miss Enid, but for now we both need a rest. In the meantime, we've promised to stay in touch, as all close friends do.

For the next year or so, I'll be writing short fiction, and you might see Roo (*The Fifth Stone*) and Ginger, the *Tri-County Gazette* office manager, show up from time to time. And it's anyone's guess where Josh may end up as a small-town police chief with his own stories to tell. And Jack, every woman's favorite character, may also drop in occasionally. So stay tuned and buckle up.

ACKNOWLEDGMENTS

First, I want to thank you, my readers, for hanging in there during this incredibly difficult year. Your loyalty and interest in the Enid Blackwell series is appreciated!

Writing a book is hard work, and I couldn't do it without a lot of help. I may be the writer, but my support team makes it possible. My husband is my number one cheerleader, my "roadie" (as he calls himself), and an inspiration for many of my stories and plot points when I get stuck. He also manages our household while I hide in my office making stuff up. I could not do what I do without his love and support.

I'd also like to thank my sister, Jane Cook, to whom this book is dedicated. She helps me in many ways—all of which I appreciate more than I've ever told her.

Major Harry Polis of the Richland County Sheriff's Department has provided invaluable police procedural research information for two of my books, including this one. I am fortunate to have Harry on my support team.

A big thanks also goes to Martha Anderson and Irene Stern who were beta readers. Both are mystery connoisseurs and provided valuable feedback on my manuscript, as well as the book cover and title.

Irene is also my incredible proofreader. She is "head mechanic" at her company, The Novel Mechanic, which provides proofreading and other services to authors like me. She is also a neighbor and friend. Together, we have solved most of the world's problems over a few glasses of wine on my porch.

And finally, I want to thank my new editor, JoAnne Scuderi, who was recommended to me by my friend and fellow author Sally Handley. After my previous editor died in 2020, I felt adrift without her support. But when I talked to JoAnne, I knew we would be able to work together. Even though she came in on the fifth novel of a series, she "got" the characters and the story I was trying to tell and provided valuable guidance. I'm glad she's on my team.

If I've left anyone out, please know that I appreciate all my friends, family, and others who have been on this incredible journey with me.

ABOUT THE AUTHOR

RAEGAN TELLER is the award-winning author of the Enid Blackwell series. *Murder in Madden* (Pondhawk Press, 2016) was her debut novel, followed by *The Last Sale* (2018), *Secrets Never Told* (2019), and *The Fifth Stone* (2020). Two of her novels received Honorable Mention  in the Writer's Digest Self-Published Book Awards, receiving judges' comments like "one of the best I've read this year," "great job combining plot and character," and "great storyteller."

Teller's mystery novels are set in and around Columbia, South Carolina, where she lives with her husband and two cats. Teller writes about small-town intrigue, family secrets, and tales of murder, and while her books are fiction, each book was inspired by an actual event.

Her short story, "The Great Negotiator," was included in the Sisters in Crime Guppies' anthology *Fishy Business* (2019). She was also a contributing author to Richland Library's make-your-own-adventure book, *It's About Time* (2018).

She is a summa cum laude graduate of Queens University, Charlotte, and a member of Sisters in Crime, South Carolina Writers Association, and the Charlotte Writers Club. https://RaeganTeller.com

Made in the USA
Columbia, SC
13 August 2021

43024599R00162